MURDER AND GRITS

COMPLETE SAVORY MYSTERY SERIES
COLLECTION; A PIPER SANDSTONE CULINARY
COZY MYSTERY

KAREN MCSPADE

NEWCASTLE
MEDIA

~

To my mother, Ruth, thank you for teaching me that love and a sense of adventure need no boundaries.
To my Italian grandmother, Noni, whose love for cooking and joyful laughter will always keep my heart full.

~

FREE GIFT

Receive your FREE copy of **Hash Browns And Homicide**, the series prequel, and get notified via email of new releases, giveaways, contests, cover reveals, and insider fun when you sign up to my VIP mailing list!

Scan Barcode To Sign Up and Claim Your FREE Exclusive Book

DESCRIPTION

For the best reading experience, start with the series prequel, *Hash Browns and Homicide* (your free gift), and then into *Murder and Grits, The Complete Savory Mystery Series (includes all five books in the series)*.

Going undercover is about to get complicated...

She's a Chicago detective hiding in a Gulf Coast town. When a dognapping and murder shake up the local community, Piper Sandstone finds herself tangled in the mystery. Now, keeping a low profile is not an option if she wants to survive.

After solving a case involving dirty cops in Chicago, Piper is forced to hide out in Savory, Alabama, until the corrupt officers land behind bars.

Better known as Alligator Alley, Savory is not your typical tourist Gulf Coast town. Why? Because it's home to three-time AKC champion poodle Victory Cup Valentino, but this year bad things are about to go down. Even before Piper can get unpacked, the poodle and his handler go missing right before the Westminster Dog Show.

Suspicions run high, especially when two other newcomers with very sketchy backgrounds show up in town. But before Piper can get any answers, all hell breaks loose when a body turns up in the bayou. And she's at the center of the crime scene.

Fortunately for Piper, a group of retired ladies known as the Dentures and Diamonds Crime Squad is on her side, and they are a force to be reckoned with. Now, they must work together to solve the crime and stop the murderer before they end up in a body bag.

Savory Mystery Series is a fun, thrilling cozy mystery adventure that will keep you riveted to your seat with twists and turns that you won't see coming.

MURDER AND GRITS

A Piper Sandstone Savory Mystery Series, Part 1

By: Karen McSpade

Edited by Darci Heikkinen

Cover Design by Rizwan Noor

PROLOGUE

A part of it was thrilling and another scary. I had never had a pair of handcuffs around my wrists before. They dug into my skin, and even though I knew there was no evidence to put me behind bars, I felt incarcerated.

Relax, Piper. He just wants to bluff, have you spill all your secrets, and give you a pat on the head. Jake is one of the good cops. I told myself these things, but I did not feel any safer when I heard the door to the office open behind me. Though he was a small-town sheriff, he had a few good interrogation techniques up his sleeve. The "wait" was one of them—and it was tiring me.

Sheriff Jake Johnson walked into the room with two cups of steaming hot coffee in his hands and set them on the desk in front of me. His angry boyish face stared at me, hoping to make me talk. I wasn't going to. I was much more disciplined than that, and he was going to be the first person in the little town to find that out.

"Do you know why I picked you up?" Jake finally spoke.

"No," I lied. I knew why he'd brought me into his barely

furnished office. It was because I had done a few things I shouldn't have done and been in a few places I shouldn't have been, and now, I was a suspect.

"Everywhere something goes wrong in this town, there you are, Sharon. You're there when I get to a crime scene. You're asking people questions, upsetting them in their own homes. You are disrupting my town," Jake said, his eyes burning with fury.

I could not tell him the truth. No one could handle the truth, not even the entire town could have handled the truth.

"Am I being arrested for something here, Jake?"

He paused and glared at me again, and I knew that was what we would be doing all day. He was trying to rattle me.

"You come into my town, and suddenly, all hell breaks loose. People get into fights around you. We've got a missing person—"

"Animal," I corrected him. "Missing animal, not person. Technically... speaking."

Anger flashed across Jake's face and left his cheeks flushed. I was sure that he hated my calm demeanor, but it was necessary. I had to prove my innocence.

"There are no records of you anywhere. I checked with a colleague of mine up in Montgomery. He couldn't find anything on you. Now, tell me who you really are, Sharon. Why have you come to my town? No more BS." His steel-blue eyes and dark brows pierced through my tough girl façade and made me want to spill everything. The fact that I even considered this for one brief second made me want to punch him.

The truth was, I couldn't tell anyone anything, or else I might end up dead.

1

WELCOME TO SAVORY

What in the name of Sherlock Holmes was Chief Hobbs thinking?

I looked around at the small bungalow—all yellowing floral wallpaper and wooden beam ceilings. Every other plank on the floor creaked when I stepped on it, and the brass light fixtures flickered at random. Everything was probably about two hundred years old and smelled of mothballs that grew their *own* mothballs. The whole place would have been charming if it weren't so damn creepy.

There's a nice little wrap-around porch, though. I liked that.

I felt a fly buzz around my ear, and I flailed my arm around to try and thwack it. Ah, yes, which reminded me. The bayou was also full of giant mosquitoes with drills for blood-suckers. Because the chief couldn't have put me in a nice city where I could have a tiny normal apartment. Oh, no. I had to hide out here in a haunted house in the middle of a damn *swamp* in Savory—what kind of name is that anyway —Alabama.

That wasn't even the worst part. That honor went to this brown, floppy-eared little thing staring at me from the corner of the living room.

A dog. Because, of course, I had to have a dog. I can't even feed myself sometimes, and now I have to feed this creature too. And he/she/it, whatever it was, had started sniffing around the large box containing my shoes. Which it probably thought were chew toys.

"Excuse me! Hey, mister!" I said. I put my hands on my hips and tried to look as menacing as possible.

The thing must have understood me because it stopped snooping around my stuff and stared right at me with those big chocolate brown eyes. Then it tilted its head at me like it was waiting for me to speak.

Oh. Okay, I did not expect that.

"Erm, okay. Is that your name, then? Mister?"

It responded with a slight wag of its tail which turned to a loud thud on the wooden floor. And then it sauntered off to the side door and into the backyard, tongue out and panting slightly.

"Okay, great. Good talk. Sorry to bore you."

Whatever. I didn't have time to understand the intricacies of dog language. I had to unpack and figure out this whole undercover thing. I dragged my suitcases over and heaved them onto the couch, taking out my clothes, so I could stuff them in the closet.

I was halfway through the first suitcase when I heard a commotion from outside. I peered out the open door. Of course! The damn dog was digging a hole in the ground all the way to China. Its short arms moved like a machine, sending soil flying everywhere.

"Hey! Don't mess with the damn yard!"

Obviously, it listened. Not. Just kept digging like crazy. Eh. Whatever. Not my house, not my problem.

I went back to my suitcase, folding shirts, taking out underwear, and thwacking the occasional mosquito when I heard Mister's muffled panting beside me.

Okay, so it had a ... bone in its mouth. It was long and yellowing and stained with soil. What the hell?

"What am I even supposed to do with you, huh? What is this? Where did you get this?"

As if pleased with the discovery, Mister moseyed on back outside to the hole it had dug—its tail wagging as it went. And then it looked over its shoulder like it was waiting for me to follow. I sighed and put down my pile of underwear.

Not gonna lie, I was a bit impressed. The hole was a few feet deep, and there were, um, even more bones at the bottom. Okay, probably some sort of animal. Nothing new. I spotted the shiny curve of a weird flat-shaped bone hidden under the dirt, and I reached over to take a good look.

It was nice and smooth with a longer piece attached. I pried it free from the soil with my fingers. It took me a few seconds to recognize the two hollowed-out sockets and the giant teeth from its large mouth.

Okay, alligator skull. ALLIGATOR SKULL! Alarm bells blared in my head, and I dropped the bone to the ground. It clattered on impact, a weird sickening sound. I felt a shiver run down my back, from the base of my neck all the way to my toes. Mister was still wagging its tail happily at me.

I took a deep breath and looked up to the heavens.

What in the name of Sherlock Holmes was Chief Hobbs thinking?

2

HIDING OUT IN ALLIGATOR ALLEY

The morning sun filtered through the sheer curtains and spilled across my bed. It was warm and inviting, compared to the angry skies of Chicago. The bad part was that it made me lazy, made me want to roll around in a bed of soft blankets, and fall right back to sleep. And I would have if it weren't for Mister's wet tongue licking the side of my face. *Ugh, not yet. Can't you let yourself out to pee?* His annoying whining told me that was not an option.

"Ah! Alright, alright!" I yelled in frustration before I slid out of bed to let Mister outside. "No digging! You hear me?" I should really think about leaving the doggie door open, so I can sleep in. But who knows what kind of swamp critters would sneak in during the night and devour Mister, or me, for that matter. Nope, better not to risk it!

I stumbled to the bathroom to brush my teeth and let the warm shower work its magic on my groggy eyes. I watched the steam swirl around my face and thought about my first couple of weeks at my new job.

The last time I worked as a waitress was almost a decade

ago, when I was in my early twenties. Serving up daily specials didn't get my blood pumping like working a crime scene, but it wasn't bad for a cover job. *You can do anything temporarily, Piper, and this is very temporary. You'll be heading home to Chicago before you know it.*

Time passed by more slowly in the coastal town of Savory, Alabama, than it did in the busier cities of America. This little town was ruled by tradition more than a need for profit.

I tried to arrive at the café early on most mornings because I knew the locals would be gathered outside waiting for Mr. B to unlock the doors. It was a small privately-owned seafood establishment where everyone came to have their coffee, exchange pleasantries, and enjoy the daily specials. The locals claimed it was the best seafood in all of Alabama.

I threw on a pair of tight Levi's jeans and a comfortable t-shirt and headed out onto the streets of Savory. The town sat right on the Gulf Coast, a perfect blend of tranquil blue ocean and southern bayou.

I looked out across the horizon and didn't miss the sight of skyscrapers. They had been replaced with gentle verdant hills lined with quaint craftsman-style homes that invited you to sit on their porches and sip sweet tea.

I took a deep breath to draw in the tranquillity of it all on my walk to the café. I never imagined that I might actually like Savory, and it was a pleasant surprise. Where I came from, you didn't make eye contact with strangers. Here, everyone was friendly—all twenty-five thousand of them.

"Hey, Carl," I greeted the little soccer star of the town. He was ten and had a rare gift that made me fancy the game. Despite the fact that he was quite small for his age and looked rather clumsy, he moved the ball around on the field like a young Cristiano Ronaldo, leaving the other boys chasing their tails. I usually felt awkward around children, but something about Carl made me think that maybe all kids weren't so bad.

"Hey, Sharon," he waved back before hitting the soccer ball up in the air with his knee and then popping it forward with his head into the makeshift soccer goal on his porch.

I continued on my route to the café, right past the sign that said Welcome to Alligator Alley. That's what the locals called this little section of town where a bridge crossed over a tributary of the Tombigbee River.

This was the spot where alligators were known to bask in the sun. Knowing this, I picked up my pace about five notches. *I swear if I ever stumble across an alligator here, it's not going to be pretty.* I patted my suede purse where my Sig Sauer 9mm was safely tucked away.

Walking past the local bakery, I looked through the open window and saw Mr. Bradley, who tossed me a Ciabatta roll every morning from one of the first batches. It took some practice for me to become a great catcher of buns, but by my second week, I was catching them quite well. Good enough for the minor baseball leagues, he joked. Like clockwork, Mr. Bradley whistled and gave his best throw. I caught the bun and took a bite out of it.

"Delicious!" I shouted back.

"You spoil me, Sharon," he replied.

I saw the café up ahead and quickly finished eating the delicious bread. Today, I was running a few minutes late, and our regular customers were already in their seats when I walked in.

Okay, here we go. Goodbye, Piper. Hello, Sharon. The phone rang in the kitchen just as I was tying my apron around my waist.

"Somebody gonna grab that?" Patrick, the line chef, yelled, slinging a slab of butter into a saucepan.

He looked more like a defensive tackle for the Chicago Bears than a cook, though he acted like a grouchy old man. Patrick didn't realize that I could have him on the ground crying like a baby in five seconds flat if I wanted. *Lay low, Piper, and don't do anything stupid to mess this up*—the chief's warning rang through my thoughts like a daily mantra.

I made a dash for the wall phone painted like a huge red lobster with giant orange claws.

"Crabby Clam Café, this is Sharon ... Oh, hi, Mrs. Davenport ... No, we haven't changed our name ... Uh-hmm. Yes, we're aware that the "m" on our sign is upside down, and I agree, the Crabby Claw doesn't have the same ring to it. I've got to run now, but I'll have Mr. B get right on that sign. Bye!"

Are you freaking kidding me? Is that all people have to worry about in this town? I hung up the phone and peered through the kitchen's serving window. My favorite customers were sitting in a booth by the front window.

The Delta Queens were superstar legends, at least by Savory standards. These four elderly ladies were an anomaly —an all-girl band that managed to stay together until their fifties. They were born and raised in Alabama and formed their band when in their twenties.

While on tour, a manager in New York discovered them and turned them into stars. They sang all over the south, performed on river showboat cruises, and eventually were invited to sing for the Governor of Alabama, who hailed them as the best female rock band of the south.

Ultimately, they retired in Savory when Rosemary, the lead singer, developed nodules on her vocal cords. She claimed it was her deep raspy voice that made her irresistible to men, but I believed it was the mountains of cleavage she so proudly—and readily—displayed that the men in Savory couldn't say no to.

Most of the locals in town knew this group of fun, zany retirees as the Delta Queens, but I got to see a whole other side of them, the side they liked to call the Dentures and Diamonds Crime Squad.

"Yoo-hoo, Sharon," Doris, Rosemary, Margie, and Patty Sue waved from their table in the café. I smiled and waved back before loading my tray with their coffee cups and heading over to their table.

"So, can you believe that Mrs. Peterson actually thought she could get away with taking money from the boys' soccer jersey fund?" asked Doris, the oldest one of the bunch who was responsible for cracking the case of the stolen jersey money and returning it.

"I'm as shocked as a clam shut tight. I thought Joanne was a lovely woman. You have to admit, her banana cream pie we won at bingo last month was to die for," added Margie with an innocent smile.

"Well, dumplin', everything shocks you. Always innocent until proven guilty. I swear, Margie, what are we gonna do with you?" asked Rosemary.

"Be nice, Rose. Margie just sees the best in people. You should try it sometime," Patty Sue retorted as she took a sip from her cup. "Wow, Sharon, this is the best cup of coffee I've had in a ... what's that saying? ...oh yeah, in a coon's age!" she laughed.

"I'm glad you like it," I couldn't help but laugh myself. I loved watching and listening to this fun bunch of besties bicker and scheme as they banded together to protect Savory from crime and mayhem. They were the first people to welcome me to town. I noticed when I was around them, I didn't feel so far away from home.

"C'mon sugar, sit down with us for a minute," Rosemary patted the outside of the bench.

"Oh, no, I really shouldn't. We're pretty busy this morning."

"Ah, these are just locals. They can wait a darn minute for that warm up. We've got some juicy news," Rosemary teased with a smile.

I knew Sharon shouldn't care about any juicy news, but Piper got the better of me. "Oh, okay, but just for a minute," I said and took a seat next to Rosemary.

"So, I was in the laundry room the other day when I came across the darndest secret in all of Savory," Patty Sue started. If anything happened in Savory, these women were always the first to know about it. The other three women leaned in, waiting to hear more. Patty Sue scratched her head and looked dazed.

"Well, are you gonna wait till we're all dead and buried to tell us?" Rosemary retorted, cleavage dancing above her chest.

"Give her a second to collect her thoughts, Rose," Margie petitioned.

"Oh yes, silly me!" Patty Sue laughed and continued, "So, I overheard my husband talking to Mr. Channing." Rosemary's eyes twinkled, and a smile spread across her face at the mention of his name. Mr. Winston Channing was the co-owner of several First National Banks locally, and everyone knew him as the wealthiest man in Savory.

Patty Sue leaned in closer to the ladies before she spoke the deets. Her husband was on the organizing board for the regional AKC dog show, making her the ideal spy to bring back the intel.

"Mr. Channing said Victory has been dognapped!" Patty Sue declared. There was a sharp and loud gasp in the café as everyone who heard reacted.

"Wait a minute," I interjected. "Who is Victory?"

Doris filled me in with all the details, "Why, honey, Victory Cup Valentino is the Channing's champion standard poodle. A 3-time Best in Show winner of the AKC National Championship. Victory is expected to take first place this year at the Westminster Dog Show. No telling how much that dog is worth in stud fees alone! And now someone has dognapped him? Unbelievable!"

It was clear to me now that this dog's reputation in the town took second place only to the Delta Queens.

"That's strange about Victory's disappearance. Who would steal a show dog that's so famous?" I inquired. I felt the usual tingle of a mystery waiting to be solved crawling up my arm, but I squashed it. This was a job for local law enforcement. And speak of the devil.

"Good morning, Sheriff Johnson," Doris nodded her head as he walked by our table. I jumped up and headed behind the counter.

Jake strolled into the café dressed for duty—tall black boots, hands on his waist, badge on his chest, and hat on his head. The ladies pretended they had not been discussing the biggest story in the town. They didn't want the sheriff to know that the Dentures and Diamonds Crime Squad was one step ahead of him.

Jake Johnson stood in the middle of the cafe and looked around. He could sense the unease in the air, but he decided against acknowledging it out loud. I rolled my eyes when his gaze fell on me, and he came my way.

"So, how was your night, new neighbor?" he asked as he settled on a stool at the front counter. He started such friendly conversations with me every day, which made me cringe on the inside.

Jake seemed like such a decent guy. If he knew about me, who I really was, I'm sure he wouldn't have that same damn puppy dog smile on his face. *Just smile, Piper, and act like you're freaking interested. Then he'll go away.*

But Jake asked too many questions. He wanted to know everything about me as he did with everyone in the town. *It's his job*, I reminded myself.

"It was nice. Thanks for asking. How was yours?" I asked him, trying to make polite conversation.

"Nothing too exciting. I worked late last night, so I got the chance to catch the harvest moon. Did you see how big it was?" he asked with his boyish smile that always caught me off guard.

"No, I missed it. I'm not much of a night owl." I kept my focus on Jake, though I could feel the pressure from every eye in the café not to spill any details about Victory to him. He looked back over his shoulder a few times, and I knew I was doing a terrible job. *You're better than this, Piper. You've bluffed men twice your age with more experience. What the hell is wrong with you?*

"Okay, what is going on here?" Jake finally asked everyone. I moved away from him onto the next customer.

"We want to know if you have any leads on the where-abouts of Victory," one of the regulars asked before taking a bite of his homemade orange roll the size of Texas.

"I've got—" Jake started to respond, then quickly looked

at the Delta Queens. The women hid their faces in their cups of coffee.

"I am close to finding out who did this" I listened to him speak, calming the locals as he always did, but I knew he had no leads. I could tell by the lack of confidence in his voice. With an annoyed look on his face, Jake tipped his hat to me and left the café, letting the door slam behind him.

Today I worked a split shift, breakfast and dinner, which gave me time to run home and check on Mister. That silly dog was always so happy to see me. I had to admit, he was kind of growing on me with that big slobbery smile of his.

It was 9:00 pm and time to start my closing duties. I erased the giant chalkboard on the wall and added tomorrow's daily specials, Mr. B's famous shrimp and grits, and his homemade pizza by the sea. Locals raved about these dishes and told me that they were family recipes. I made a mental note to stay for lunch tomorrow, so I could try the shrimp and grits.

"I'm out of here, Mr. B," I yelled through the kitchen window.

"Good night, Sharon. See you tomorrow," he replied.

"Don't forget to lock the damn door on your way out," Patrick yelled, waving a chef's knife in my direction. *Okay, Mr. Grumpy pants. I'm pretty sure I know where the Crabby Clam got its name.*

I enjoyed walking home after my evening shifts. The nights were always quiet and beautiful, with lights from the nearby houses fluttering onto the streets. It gave me time to relax, to shake off the façade of Sharon, and to remember who I really was.

I was halfway across town when I heard a familiar voice behind me. It was Remy. I had just passed the Tequila Mockingbird Lounge, and I could tell by his slurred speech that he had probably been kicked out again.

"Heyyyy, Sharon, Ima talking to ya!" he yelled, stumbling toward me. I always ignored him, but tonight, he came after me. I picked up my pace, but I could still hear his heavy footsteps behind me.

"You're drunk, Remy. Now, go home before you get arrested."

"What if I wanna go home with you?"

I felt his hand on my shoulder for a split second before I grabbed his wrist and turned while twisting his arm the other way to lock him in a jiu-jitsu hold.

He winced and then looked at me and smiled. "That aaall ya got, pretty lady?" Without even thinking, I took my right elbow and came down hard on his arm, nearly breaking it. He yelled, cursing at me as I took off running.

Dammit, Piper! No one can know about you! Why are you so reckless? I scolded myself as I ran. I had almost broken Remy's arm in a town like Savory, where everyone knows everything. I was certain the Dentures and Diamonds Crime Squad would be privy to the news before they graced us with their presence at the café the next morning.

Remy was drunk, and he accosted me, I reminded myself as I made my way briskly back to my bungalow. I wasn't supposed to be able to hurt a man twice my size so easily. I knew I could always lie and say it wasn't me. Which was actually the truth ... Sharon would never resort to violence. At least, that was the story I needed everyone here to believe.

I ran until I reached the safety of my place. Once inside, I closed the door and locked it behind me.

Mister jumped around playfully to greet me, clearing off the coffee table with his tail in the process. What am I going to do with you? You're a mess, I told the dog then rubbed his big floppy ears anyway.

Everything is okay. I assured both of us as I walked to the kitchen cabinet and pulled out a bottle of smooth Conecuh Ridge Whiskey that I poured into a small glass. The sting down the back of my throat brought me back to reality.

I noticed the green flashing light on my answering machine. There was only one person who ever left me messages.

"Just a friendly reminder of why you're in Savory and not in Chicago, Piper. Don't get distracted, and don't do anything stupid." Chief Hobbs's voice was serious and brief, just like his other messages.

Tonight, all I cared about was the calmness I felt at the mention of my name—my real name, Piper Sandstone.

3

NEW FACES

I t was easier to wake up on Friday mornings. Probably because I was motivated by my early morning walk with the ladies before heading into work. Our route took us down by the fishing pier and marina, where we would gawk over the fancy houseboats and yachts gently rocking back and forth with the tide.

Within minutes, I was up and dressed in a pair of sneakers, a tank top, and leggings, with my auburn hair tied up in a ponytail. I locked up and headed out onto the streets of Savory. The sky in the early morning hours was a beautiful watercolor of blue, lavender, and peach, and the roads were already filled with walkers and joggers.

"Hello, Sharon," Mr. and Mrs. Hamilton waved to me as they walked past. They were both in their eighties and walked everywhere together. They were so cute and in love. I could tell by the way they looked at each other with such adoring eyes. It was the life I had imagined for myself and Brian. But I was a fool for thinking that I was special, that he would treat me differently than all the other women he conquered before me.

Just breathe, Piper. You broke up with him, remember? I tried to remind myself of this each time I thought of his bad-boy smirk that turned me on. It was annoying that I still remembered his face, his eyes, his lips, and the feel of him. The fact that I had forgotten the combination to the gym locker we shared was the only progress I had made since I caught him with another woman. *At least you found out before you married him!*

"Sharon!" Doris called from down the street, startling me. I took a deep breath to recollect myself before jogging over to meet the ladies.

Doris was dressed nicely in a pair of loose-fitting khaki capri pants with a white button-down blouse with small pink roses embroidered down the front. She always looked so well put together, no matter where she was going.

"Good morning, ladies," I said as I joined them. "Oh, I love your matching hot pink tennis shoes with the sequins and rhinestones!"

"Oh, these old things? Well, thank you, Sugarplum. These are a throwback to our days as the Delta Queens," Rosemary smiled. She was wearing hot pink tights, a royal blue leotard with a white athletic t-shirt stretched tightly over it, and a leopard print headband. She looked like an older Olivia Newton-John from her '80s-era music video "Let's Get Physical."

"Those shoes bring back a lot of great memories. And they are comfortable too!" Margie declared as she came shuffling up from behind wearing a pair of white cotton shorts and a yellow t-shirt with a giant smiling sun in the middle and the words "Morning Sunshine!" printed in bold black letters.

I didn't want to be the one to tell Patty Sue, especially since no one else had mentioned it, that her cotton Bermuda shorts were on backwards. I couldn't help but wonder, though, if she just thought they zipped in the back.

It was great to see these four women so happy and full of life. Especially Rosemary, since her husband had passed away suddenly from a heart attack several years back.

"I adored Robert, and I can never replace him, but now that he's gone, he would want me to move on with my life and be happy," Rosemary had shared with me on a previous walk. I'd recently learned this meant that every man in Savory, young or old, was fair game.

This morning, the ladies took me on a different route, and I didn't question them. They knew Savory better than I did. They also knew what time I had to be at work, so I knew they had my back.

"Quick question, Sharon. Why haven't you made any friends since you've been here?" Patty Sue asked out of genuine curiosity. The women had taken it upon themselves to worry about my life. They asked a lot of questions which was also the reason they knew about every person in Savory.

"Well, I have you guys," I replied with my best sheepish smile.

"Yes, but you have no female friends your age," Doris added.

"And you live alone," Margie worried.

"How does a gorgeous young woman like yourself not have a boyfriend or at least a sexual partner?" Rosemary asked in disbelief. She always puffed her breasts up whenever she mentioned the word "sex," which she did a lot.

"Okay, the inquisition party is over, and you guys need to give me a break. I've only been in Savory for a couple of weeks!" I smiled to stave off their questions. They did not know who I was, not really, and they did not know about Brian. Perhaps if they did, they would have been less worried about my sex life, or they would have been like my friends in Chicago who believed that the solution to heartbreak from a man was more men.

For the next few minutes, we walked in silence, taking in all the sights and sounds around us. As we approached the rough, unkempt lawn of the Pellegrino's, the ladies stopped and stared.

"I heard they hate dogs. Our friend Lisa walked her Boxer puppy across their lawn a few days ago, and Tina cussed her out. They really hate dogs," Doris repeated.

"Tina and Mike Pellegrino moved to Savory a couple of weeks before you arrived, Sharon. They opened a dry cleaning business and bought the old car wash off Mullet Hill Road. Quite the entrepreneurs those two are," explained Margie.

"Yes, but they're not too friendly. I guess they don't like people either. Maybe that explains why they hired someone to run their businesses for them. Hmmm? Do you think they could have taken Victory?" asked Patty Sue.

"No, I don't think so. They're just cat people. I've seen Tina on the front porch with half a dozen cats hanging around. Besides, if there is any real suspicion, I'm sure Jake will question them," Doris piped in.

"Ooh, which reminds me"—Rosemary turned to me—"speaking of Sheriff Jake Johnson, I think he fancies you, Sharon. I see the way he walks into the cafe, shoulders up, chest out, ready to impress you."

Suddenly the wheels in my head started turning, but not about Jake Johnson. He was tall and handsome, and perhaps on a drunken night at a club, I wouldn't mind taking him to my bungalow, but I was off men for a while, a long while.

The wheel in my head was turning because of the case again. I had dreamed about it last night, and though I had tried to forget about it this morning, it had taken over my thoughts again.

"What did Mrs. Channing tell Jake about Victory's disappearance?" I endured the smirks on the faces of the women when I called the sheriff by his first name, but I needed to get an answer without seeming too involved.

"Valorie told him it had to be her dog's handler, Susan. Apparently, they caught her on their security cameras as she was leaving the backside of the property with Victory. So, she is the prime suspect," Doris answered.

"So, why hasn't Jake questioned this woman?" I asked.

"Well, no one's seen her since then. Susan's originally from Nashville, you see, and I'm sure Jake has made some calls to see if he can locate her. But there is only so much he can do by himself. That is why he needs the Dentures and Diamonds Crime Squad," Patty Sue said with pride.

These ladies were not the fastest walking buddies, but they had a strong track record of solving cases. I remembered them telling me how they busted the double chocolate chip cookie burglar at Carl's home.

Turns out the thief was one of his soccer teammates who lived down the street. While the family was sleeping, this little devil would sneak in through Carl's window and steal cookies from the family's kitchen.

But then he got sloppy and left a taunting note by the

cookie jar: You make the cookies. I eat them all! It was signed 'Cookie Monster.'

The Crime Squad suspected one of the kids in the neighborhood, so they had them sign up to win a free Nintendo video game. When James was told to sign the form using the words cookie monster, he took off running and eventually confessed.

The ladies had beamed with confidence as they shared their victory with me, but I feared they did not realize that Victory's disappearance was a whole different ball game. I also worried there was more that would soon turn up.

My mind had drifted so far away that I had not noticed we had stopped again.

"Speak of Adonis, and he appears," Rosemary beamed. "You have to admit, Sharon, he looks pretty hot in uniform."

I looked up and saw Jake Johnson a few houses away from us talking to Mrs. Blackwell. They were standing in her driveway, her Cairn Terrier sitting by her side. I knew instinctively why he was there. The ladies told me everything.

The Blackwell's dog, Murphy's Magic Oil, was a close rival of Victory's and had come in second place in the regional AKC dog show the past two years. They had motive, but I could tell that Jake was going about his questioning the wrong way.

"Jake is too blunt. He's a good man, though," Rosemary said, still selling him to me as though she had read my mind. "But he is too blunt. He hasn't the tiniest clue about talking to women. He'll never get anyone to talk," she said.

I agreed. Watching him, I could see that he was fighting a lost battle. I felt anxious for him, but I turned away from the scene. *Don't get involved. Anytime you get involved, Piper, people get hurt.* I reminded myself.

I turned back, and our eyes met. Though Jake did not smile, I could almost see what Rosemary had said earlier. His shoulders seemed raised, and his chest was puffed up as he looked at us. He thanked Mrs. Blackwell and patted Murphy on the head, nodding to us before getting into his truck.

"That was either to me, or it was to you, Sharon. You better tie that fine young man down before I do it myself," Rosemary said. We all broke into laughter.

They were good company, and I was trying to stay in the world they lived in. I tried not to worry so much about the missing dog. *After all, Sharon would leave this case in the hands of the law, but what about Piper Sandstone?* I knew I had to be careful.

A hot shower after a long walk always put me in the mood to sleep, but I fought it. Though this wasn't my real life, it was my life at the moment, and I needed to continue until I was summoned home. I checked my voicemail, but there was nothing new. It was disappointing but not unexpected.

I arrived at the café, and the Delta Queens were already there. They greeted me as though we had not seen each other earlier that morning. As I turned toward their table with their coffee, a tall man with blond hair came up to the counter and pulled out his wallet.

"Good morning, can I get a menu?" the man asked with a thick Texan accent.

"Sorry, I have to attend to the ladies first, but the specials are listed on the board" I cut him off politely.

"Is that the way you people treat new customers around here?" he asked me.

"You're new to Savory. Georgia?" I pried.

His face beamed. "How did you know?" he asked, losing the Texan accent.

"Just a good hunch. And your wallet has the University of Georgia logo." I answered, trying to hide my unease. He was a liar and an unusually good one. My mind asked the obvious questions; who is this guy, and why did he try to fool me with that Texan accent?

"You're an intuitive woman," he remarked. "And you are certainly more polite than your sheriff."

"Jake is a ... uh, please excuse me." I walked away to serve the ladies.

"Who is that man? We've never seen him here before," Doris asked.

"I don't know, but I'm going to find out," I promised them before heading back to the counter.

"The sheriff just wants to keep everyone safe, so he is a little standoffish with strangers, but don't you worry, you'll like him once you get to know him," I told the man.

"I'm Adam. Adam Kane. What's your name?"

"Sharon," I replied, watching his eyes. There was no suspicion in his big green eyes, but I still wondered.

"So, what brings you to Alligator Alley, Adam?'

"Alligator what?" he asked. *Well, he obviously hasn't been here long because he doesn't know the town's nickname, and the Delta Queens don't know him.*

A sudden sense of panic fluttered in my stomach and made my throat dry up. *What if he's from Chicago, and he's down here to take me out? The police force had a vast network, and it wouldn't be impossible for someone to find me here. Crap, Piper!* I wanted to run, but I forced myself to stay.

"How are the shrimp and grits here?" Adam inquired.

"Delicious," I choked out, trying to breathe.

"Perfect. I'll take that to go. Thanks, Sharon." He smiled.

I ran back to the kitchen. "Hey, Patrick. The guy at the counter needs an order of shrimp and grits to go. I've got to run. I'm not feeling well."

"Damn, Sharon, you can't just walk out in the freaking middle of your shift! Don't even try that 'it's a girl thing' either. That won't fly around here!" he threatened with a hot pan in his hand.

But I was already headed out the door. I didn't even bother to say goodbye to the ladies, and I knew they would ask what happened. I couldn't tell them my suspicions about Adam without telling them who I really was. I feared the truth about Piper Sandstone would be too much for them to bear. I couldn't handle the look of disappointment and betrayal on their faces if they found out I was lying to them, regardless of the reason.

I ran all the way back to my bungalow and didn't stop until I was safely inside. I leaned over to catch my breath. My temples were throbbing. *Who the hell are you, Adam? And why have you come to Savory?*

I went into my bedroom and grabbed my Sig Sauer out of my nightstand, checking to make sure it was loaded. Then I sank into the couch, welcoming the feel of the cold steel resting in my hands.

4

PATTY SUE SUSPECTS

S ummer in Alligator Alley was brutal. The afternoon sun and humidity made tiny beads of sweat form on my upper lip. There was no sense in wearing makeup. Rosemary was the only woman I had seen pull it off successfully, and I'm pretty sure she sprayed a thin coat of clear epoxy on her face to hold her makeup in place. I just couldn't bring myself to fight the weather here. Fighting the vampire mosquitos in the bayou was hard enough.

Life was different in many ways here compared to living in the suburbs of Chicago. I could walk most places I wanted to go in Savory, so I rarely had to pull my loaner Mustang out of the garage. It wasn't as nice as my Hemi, that's for sure, but at least it was fast.

I was headed to the outskirts of town to visit Patty Sue on Friday evening. She and her husband bought a new TV, and they needed some help setting it up. She asked for my assistance because she wasn't technical enough to do it, and "Herb has the patience and attention span of a two-year-old," she laughed. I told her I was happy to help. It was the least I could do.

As I drove past the bakery, I could see candlelight filtering through the store window and a closed sign on the door. It was the Bradley's wedding anniversary, and he was having dinner with his wife. Seeing that he didn't have time to head home, along with Mr. Bradley's fear that his wife would fall asleep at the sight of a bed, I had advised that he set the dinner celebration at the bakery to surprise her. Knowing thoughtful Mr. Bradley, it was bound to be a successful date.

Getting to witness moments like this where life seemed less rushed and more cherished made Savory and its residents feel special. Folks in this town didn't need to look hard to find a reason to celebrate.

The Delta Queens had asked me about my birthday several times, and I had always changed the subject. I knew I could not do it forever, but the thought of a crowd at my place or people singing to me at the café made me shudder. I was not the kind of girl who craved being the center of attention.

I arrived at Patty Sue's house and pulled into the driveway. Like many houses on the edge of town, hers had no fence. Bright raspberry crepe myrtles framed the house on either side, and the front was lined with white rhododendrons and yellow calla lilies. The house was shaded by a thirty-foot-tall black tupelo tree with the most beautiful apricot and reddish-green leaves. I took a minute to marvel at her landscape before knocking on the front door.

I could hear Patty Sue bouncing toward the door, and she answered it with such force it almost sucked me into the house.

"Sharon, right on time. Get on in here!" she said, holding the door open for me.

"Hi, Patty Sue," I said as I followed her inside.

It was the first time I had been in any of the women's houses, and Patty Sue's was like a trip down memory lane. Photos of her in her younger years and all kinds of Delta Queens merchandise filled the large sitting room. Framed album covers decorated the wall on either side of the large gold framed mirror above a pink antique sofa. One picture, in particular, caught my eye, and I walked over for a closer look.

Patty Sue was in the middle holding a pair of drumsticks. Rosemary was to her right, blowing a kiss with her hands under her breasts. Doris stood defiantly with her hands on her hips, and Margie almost disappeared into the background. These women had never changed. I realized why they enjoyed such a successful career. They were the Delta Queens through and through.

"We were pretty back then, weren't we?" she said, standing in front of one of the large photos that had the 30-something-year-old women dressed like rock stars.

"You still are," I replied, and I meant it.

"Aw, you are as sweet as my mama's apple pie," she said. I saw that she needed to hear those words, which made me happy. "Well, enough reminiscing about the past," she said as she led me to the adjoining room. "The television is over there. My husband got it about two weeks ago, and neither of us has been able to operate the darn thing. It is like a computer or something."

"Of course, let me take a look at it." I was a little surprised they didn't ask one of their neighbors for help. Either Patty Sue believed everyone from Chicago was more tech-savvy, or she wanted to see me for other reasons. I had a feeling it was the latter.

"Where is the remote control?" I asked. She pointed to the

small end table next to the sofa. I picked up the remote and turned the TV on. I could feel her eyes on me as I worked the controller to pick the correct settings for the television.

"You want to find Victory, don't you?" she suddenly asked me.

"I don't," I yelled abruptly before I realized how wrong that had sounded. "I do, but it's not my place. I mean ... we have a sheriff, and he is doing his best to find the dog. I am sure it will turn up eventually."

It was easy to get into character, falling back so that others could take the spotlight. It was a requirement for my previous job in the city, where I assisted senior detectives with egos as big as the Sears Tower. I rarely received credit for my work, and as much as I hated it, the chief warned me not to take it personally. "Your day is coming, Piper, I promise you," he reminded me.

Patty Sue's response jarred me back, "That's hogwash. I don't think you believe a word you just said, and neither do I. We like you, Sharon. There is something very special about you. We can see it in you, even if you can't. And I'm willing to bet over Herb's dead body that you want to find Victory as much as we do," Patty Sue declared as though she had read my palms.

"Well, of course, I am curious to know what happened to Victory," I tried to wiggle my way out.

"Now that's *my* girl!" Patty exclaimed. "Now, let me fill you in on what we know so far. People say the Channings saw the dog handler leaving the property with Victory on their security cameras, and they showed the footage to Jake when he interviewed them. But I know Susan. She's a lovely person. She doesn't seem the type to take off with Victory. And what's her motive?"

"Maybe she felt sorry for the dog? Thought Victory wasn't being treated well?" I asked.

"Not a chance. The Channings treat that dog like royalty. Probably because they couldn't have their own children, I reckon."

"Well, let's just assume for a minute that Susan did take Victory. Where would she take him?" I wondered aloud. "I mean, she couldn't be hiding in Savory with a big white very-recognizable champion poodle, right?"

"If she did take Victory, then she's probably up in Montgomery, where she lived before she moved here. But I don't think she would commit a crime like this. It just doesn't make sense," Patty added.

"Well, who else in the town would have any reason to steal a famous show dog?" I prodded for more information. "Do you think the Channings could be lying? Although that doesn't make much sense either."

"No. The Channings are extremely wealthy and a little too uppity for me, but I don't think they would lie. What would they even have to gain?" wondered Patty Sue. "The only other suspects we've got are the reclusive Pellegrinos, the competitive Blackwells, and that guy that came into the restaurant the other day, Adam Kane. Both the Pellegrinos and Kane are new to town, and we don't know much about them."

"True. But I'm also new to town. You don't suspect me, do you?" I asked with a playful wink.

"Sugar dumplin', if you can hide a huge standard poodle in that tiny bungalow of yours, you have got the whole town fooled." We both laughed at the ridiculous thought of it.

I taught Patty Sue how to use her television and the fancy new remote. Then she strongarmed me into joining her and Herb for supper before I was allowed to head home.

I was a couple of blocks away from my place when I noticed an unusual black sedan parked on the opposite side of the road. I knew all the cars in the neighborhood from my daily runs, so I slowed down to get a better look. This was a car I hadn't seen around in the area before. I would have driven past without a second look had I not seen the blond hair of the driver.

It was Adam Kane. He was talking to a woman in the driver's seat. She had long blonde hair draped around her shoulders, so I couldn't get a good look at her face. As soon as she noticed me staring in her direction, she covered her face with a sun hat. Adam suddenly turned and watched me drive by. This time he wasn't smiling.

I hit the gas and sped off. *It's none of your business, Piper.* But that same feeling of fear started burning in my stomach. I decided it was best not to drive home till I could be sure that he wasn't following me. I pulled my purse close to me and reached inside. I felt my 9mm pistol and pulled it out of its holster. *Try coming after me, Adam, and you will be sorry.*

I drove around town until I was certain I wasn't being followed. It was now well after nine o'clock, and I was ready to get home. I was craving a shot of whiskey, to feel the burn of it in the back of my throat instead of the fear.

As I circled back around toward my place, I approached the Pellegrino's house. Even in the dark, I could see Mike Pellegrino standing along the side of the house in muddy boots with a shovel in his hands. From what I could tell, he had buried something—but what had he buried?

~

A loud ring startled me from my sleep. I reached over Mister and slapped my alarm. RING! RING! *Oh, hell, it's the phone, Piper, answer it!* Without opening my eyes, I grabbed the phone on my nightstand.

"Hello," I whispered.

"Wake up, Buttercup, time to rise and shine," said Margie, sounding more chipper than usual.

"Oh, hi, Margie," I tried my best to shake myself out of the fog I was in.

"It's 9:00 am, and I'm calling to make sure you're up and getting dressed. We want you to come to church with us today."

"Oh ... church?" I tried my best to come up with an excuse, but I was too sleepy to think that quickly.

I quit going to church in Chicago when my then fiancé, Brian, refused to continue going with me because he was always too busy. I got tired of answering questions and making excuses for him, so I didn't go back. But, of course, I couldn't tell Margie any of this.

"I'm not sure I have anything to wear," I uttered, hoping she would take the hint.

"What do you mean? I know you have a pair of jeans and a nice blouse. You don't have to be all dressed up to go to church in this town. Sweetie, God loves you just the way you are, tattoos and all!" Margie exclaimed before continuing. "Truly, Sharon, you're so beautiful you could wear a gunny-sack and stop people dead in their tracks. Now get up and get dressed, and we'll stop by at ten am sharp to pick you up. See you soon!" and Margie hung up before I had a chance to reply.

I laid there for a brief moment with the receiver on my breasts and patted Mister's head. *Uggh! Why me?* Piper did not want to go to church. But Sharon knew I had to. So, I rolled my naked body out of bed and sauntered over to my wreck of a closet and started digging through it.

I managed to locate the only sundress that made the trip with me. It was wrinkled and smelled like mothballs, but it would have to do. I plucked it from the closet and headed to the bathroom to see what I could do with the bird's nest of hair that was sitting on top of my head.

The Delta Queens loved Sundays in Savory. They enjoyed getting to see all the kids and visit with everyone. Personally, I'd never been a fan of crowds of strangers. It was different here, though. The folks in this town were happy to see each other, and some curious part of me I didn't recognize longed to share in that happiness with them.

The sermon was quick; a little about the gospel and a little about the good citizens of Savory who were willing to lend a hand to a neighbor in need. The preacher knew everyone by name. Before the service was over, he asked the Channing's to come to the pulpit so they could make a plea to the folks to help them find Victory. While everyone was moved, I seemed to be the only one in shock. The petite and beautiful Mrs. Channing was the woman I had seen in the car with Adam Kane on Friday night.

5

STRANGER DANGER

I awoke early the following Monday, my mind whirling with questions. I thought about Valorie Channing and the mysterious Adam Kane. They obviously knew one another, but what did that mean? And why did Valorie not want me to see her face? Was Adam a private investigator she hired to help find Victory? That could spell trouble for me. Who was Adam Kane, and what was his connection with Valorie? Whatever it was, it was secretive, and I did not like it.

It's not your business. I told myself and got out of bed. I wasn't in the mood to go outside, so I got down on my hands and toes and did twenty-five push-ups. My muscles were still in perfect shape.

Some days, I thought it was futile to hold onto the hope my arms might still be of any use other than for serving up Mr. B's savory seafood dishes. Despite the serenity of this little gulf coast town, I wanted more. I longed for action, for purpose, for the feel of a gun at my side. For Piper's sake, I held onto this hope.

I had a shower and was about to head out when I noticed

a message on my answering machine. This time the stern male voice conveyed a sense of urgency.

"Piper, how soon can you get to Chicago?"

I could not believe my ears. My legs became so weak that I plopped down on my sofa to avoid falling. It had been weeks, and I had started to think I was never going to get back to my previous life. I was finally being summoned to Chicago.

I called my boss at the café to let him know I had an emergency situation. Mr. B was understanding, as usual, said he would call Carla in to pick up my shift. He wished me well and then hung up.

The drive to Chicago was a straight shot. I was looking forward to making the road trip with my hair blowing in the wind, singing a little too loud to Jason Aldean, who the Delta Queens turned me onto. "You can't live in Alabama without listening to a little country music, Sharon!" Doris exclaimed.

I jumped in my Mustang and fired her up. Then I headed toward the other side of town to catch the main highway. There were plenty of surprised faces as I drove through the familiar streets of Savory because people were used to seeing me walk everywhere. As I drove past the Crabby Clam Café, a few of the locals recognized me and waved. *Surprise, guys, I will not be in today and perhaps not tomorrow, or perhaps not ever again. Who knows? Chicago knows.*

I was approaching the entrance ramp to the highway when I noticed a car behind me. It didn't have its blinker on, but it turned and followed me up the ramp. I didn't think much of it at first. But then I noticed it was still behind me when I was almost an hour outside of town. It was just far enough behind me that I couldn't tell what kind of car it was or get a good look at the driver.

I sped up. I noticed the dark car in my rearview mirror sped up too. I slowed down. The car behind me slowed down, keeping the same distance between us. *Okay, you creep, why are you tailing me?* As a test, I decided to pull over on the side of the highway. Before I slowed down, I pulled my pistol out from under the seat and slid it under my right thigh.

As I expected, the car slowed down and pulled over behind me. After a few seconds, the driver's door opened, and out came Adam Kane. His tall, lanky frame was rather intimidating as he walked over to my car. He was wearing a pair of nice khaki pants and a white button-down Oxford shirt with his blond hair combed and slicked back. He did not look dressed to kill, which was a reassuring sign, although my nerves were telling a different story.

He approached my window, which I hadn't been quick enough to roll up, and leaned in on his elbows, uncomfortably close.

"Hey there, stranger. I thought that was you. Are you having car problems?"

"No ... I, uh, I pulled over to find another playlist," I lied, realizing that I didn't even have my cell phone anymore.

"Oh. Where you headed?" he asked, peering into my vehicle.

"Home. I'm going back home. I enjoyed my visit to Savory, though. May even come back someday," I said with the sweetest smile I could muster. "You?"

"Oh, I'm going to visit an old friend in Montgomery, so I guess I'll be right behind you for a ways." He kept his eyes on mine as he spoke.

"Well, that's good ... I mean, if I run into any car trouble," I bluffed and slid my leg to make sure the gun was fully covered.

"So, I saw you in church yesterday. When Valorie Channing got up to speak, you looked like you'd seen a ghost. Did you see a ghost, Sharon?" he asked in a slow threatening voice, emphasizing my name at the end. It was a question that was as clear as it was vague. *Play it cool, Piper.*

"No," I laughed. "I was just blown away by how beautiful Mrs. Channing is. I'd never seen her before, and she is stunning," I lied, hoping he was buying my bluff. It must have worked because the friendly tone in his voice returned when he realized I didn't recognize her.

"Well, I'll let you get back on your way," he patted my window ledge with both hands. "If you need anything, I'll be right behind you. Till Montgomery anyway." He got back in his car and waited for me to pull out first. I started my engine and sped up to pull onto the highway. Adam Kane wasn't far behind me.

Geez! That was way too close for comfort! I tried to slow my breathing down, but my heart rate was not cooperating. *Who the hell are you, Adam? And what is your connection to Valorie Channing?* I was determined to find out. I had to admit that Savory was going to get more complicated by the time I returned—if I returned.

There were many people in Chicago, after all, who still wished me dead.

RED BEANS AND R.I.P

A Piper Sandstone Savory Mystery Series, Part 2

By: Karen McSpade

NEWCASTLE MEDIA

Edited by Darci Heikkinen

Cover Design by Rizwan Noor

6

COMPLICATIONS

The excitement I felt about heading home to Chicago was squashed by my unexpected visitor. Despite Taylor Swift blasting on my car stereo, I felt a cold dread creeping up the back of my neck. I checked my rearview mirror every five seconds even though I knew Adam Kane got on the I-65 to Montgomery hours ago. My palms hurt from holding the steering wheel in a death grip. What was he up to?

C'mon, shake it off, Piper. He's just freaking you out. Intimidation tactics and all that.

Yes. Taylor Swift. I needed to focus on the music. And Chicago. I was less than fifteen minutes away.

I sang along to Taylor, belting out "You Belong With Me," keeping thoughts of Adam Kane and his golden hair far, far away. Instead, I thought of what I'd be doing in Chicago. My meeting with the chief was still a mystery. I didn't get much from his short and stern-sounding voicemail.

"Piper, how soon can you get to Chicago?" was the only

thing the voicemail said. But he may as well have said I won the lottery with the way my heart leaped up in my chest.

Maybe Chief Hobbs had good news for me. Maybe I'd be returning soon!

That was good...right?

I mean, I'd get back to my good ol' city life! Back to big, crazy Chicago. Back to the precinct where I belonged. Back to the action as Detective Piper Sandstone! Away from the giant mosquitos of Savory. And the weird disappearances. And the quaint, sleepy smallness of that town.

But then...I'd have to say goodbye to the Dentures and Diamonds Crime Squad, wouldn't I? And to the Crabby Clam Café?

The thought made my stomach flip, so I set it aside, along with the mysterious Adam Kane.

As I rolled into the city, I found Chicago just as vibrant as I left it—the streets buzzing with action as I hit rush hour traffic. Car horns honked every five seconds. Sirens blared, and clouds of exhaust wheezed out in a dark grey blur. People rushed around to catch the L train. If this were another time, I would have been annoyed with the whole thing, the traffic, the noise, the polluted sky.

But right now, I realized just how much I missed it.

I made a few quick turns and found myself in front of the precinct once again. My home. The towering red brick building beckoned me over, and I reminded myself to park a good distance away lest a former colleague see me. My disguise wasn't much, just a funky-looking blonde wig and dark shades. All the more reason to be careful.

It was two minutes past six. I knew he'd be out soon. There was nothing else for me to do but sit and wait.

Like clockwork, Chief Hobbs came out of the building,

looking like an honorable officer in his uniform and blazer. He got in his car, an inconspicuous Ford Focus, and pulled out onto the road.

I followed him closely and flashed my lights, so he would know I was behind him. I knew he wanted to talk when he turned away from his usual route and drove for the mall closest to the precinct.

He slowed to a stop in an empty parking space, and I drove in next to him.

"You shouldn't have come," he says, even before his window was rolled down completely.

"You asked me to," I counter before he could raise his voice.

"I sent you another message this morning telling you not to come."

"What? Well, I didn't get it. Obviously."

He sighed and trained his gaze on the shopping mall.

"Impatient as always," he said, looking tired all of a sudden. "The trial was moved forward again. I spoke with the judge. It's best that you remain in Savory until the trial date. Lay low for the time being," He wouldn't even look at me as he said this.

"What? You mean I can't come back yet?" I raised my voice at him, but he stayed still, unshaken.

When he didn't answer, I tried again. "How long?"

"It might take...a while."

"A WHILE? That's all you got for me? A while!"

"Detective Sandstone, control yourself," he said, his voice steely. His eyes swiveled from left to right, making sure no civilians were within earshot of us.

"I did the right thing! I did everything that was asked of me! So, why is it me who has to run?"

"You did *not* do the right thing," he snarled, snapping his head toward me. "Or have you forgotten?"

Well, I didn't really know what to say to that. So, yes, maybe I was a hothead. I couldn't help it. The dirty cops were right there! Of course, I wanted to take them down. It was the only logical thing to do.

"It's no longer a police case, Piper. It's politics now. These cops are well connected and extremely dangerous." he continues. "So, let me handle this, okay? I need you to trust me. Soon, I promise, you'll be back in Chicago," he said in his soothing low voice.

My eyes pricked with embarrassment. It felt like I was the naughty officer who got put on a time-out while everyone in the precinct laughed at me. I crossed my arms and stared at the mall to hide the tears forming in my eyes.

"I need you to trust me on this, Piper. I promise you; I will do whatever it takes to fix this. Whatever it takes. I promised my sister and your father I would look after you. And I will honor that promise."

At the mention of my father, I cringed with shame. I imagined he was so filled with disappointment and embarrassment that he wouldn't allow the mention of my name in his presence. Way to go, Piper!

I started my car engine, and without looking back, I nodded in agreement to trust my uncle. What other choice did I even have?

"Don't do anything stupid when you get back to Savory," he called out to me, like an afterthought.

But I was already gone.

～

Morgan's studio apartment was small and cozy, and meticulously clean. There were rows of perfectly lined books on the shelves and thriving potted plants by the windowsill.

I was not quite sure if Morgan remembered handing me his spare key years ago. Since his apartment was closer to the precinct than mine, we always ended up hanging out at his place. Mine was always too messy, anyway, and not up to his insane standards. One time, he ended up cleaning my whole apartment because it made him feel itchy.

The lights were off, which was perfect. Just the glow of the afternoon sunlight streamed in through the windows. So, I sat in the shadows and waited.

Pretty soon, a key turned in the lock, and Morgan stepped into the apartment.

"Hey, Chipmunk."

"Aaaah!" he yelped, jumping a mile high and clutching at his chest. "What the hell? Piper?"

I broke out into a grin and leaped off the sofa, crushing him with a bear hug.

"Missed ya, Chipmunk! You shoulda seen your face!"

"What the hell is wrong with you? You almost gave me a heart attack!"

"Came for a visit." I tussled at his messy hair. His face still looked pale, like all the blood had drained from his head.

"Obviously," he said, rolling his eyes. "What are you doing here? Are you even allowed to be here?"

"Chief called me back to Chicago. Well, kind of. Let's just say there was a misunderstanding."

He scrutinized me carefully, and I remembered I'm still wearing the flimsy disguise. I whipped off the blonde wig and started fiddling with one of his plants on the windowsill, a pretty-looking succulent I would have killed in a week.

The whole meeting with Chief Hobbs was annoying and disappointing. I was literally vibrating with excitement and... hope when I heard his message. Hope that my life would finally get back to normal. And to have all of that crushed in the span of less than five minutes? Not so great.

"He thinks it'll be a while before I can come back," I mumbled, my way of explanation. Morgan picked up on my morose tone and diverted the topic instead.

"Ah, well. Nothing much going on around here, either."

I knew for a fact that was not true. New York City probably had the title, but Chicago never slept either. I was thankful for the diversion, nonetheless.

"How's life in Sourpatch, Alabama?"

"It's Savory, you idiot."

I filled Morgan in on my life in Alabama. The fabulous adventures of the Dentures and Diamonds Crime Squad. The even more fabulous adventures of Sharon the waitress, aka me. The curious case of the missing show dog. The trainer who mysteriously ran off. The Pellegrinos and the Channings and everything about them that I couldn't figure out. Like a word that sat just on the tip of my tongue that I couldn't quite grasp. I told him about Sheriff Jake Johnson and the elusive Adam Kane.

Speaking of...

"Adam Kane. Can you run a background check on him?"

"Think he's a detective too?"

"I'm not sure. But he's hiding something, I can tell. And he tailed me on the way here. Well, part of the way. There's just... something, you know? Underneath all that bravado that I can't quite put my finger on."

"Well," he says, stretching out his arms and reaching for his laptop. "A regular forensic scientist would tell you that running a background check outside of the precinct is damn near impossible."

I winked at him. He was clearly enjoying this.

"Well, you're obviously not a regular forensic scientist, right?"

"Nope! I can access the server from here," he says with a grin.

He started clicking and clacking away at his laptop until a database containing Adam Kane's files showed up on the screen, file upon file popping up like mushrooms.

"Whoa. Okay, we got a hit. He has a record."

"Really? Let me see!"

As the files loaded on the laptop, my mind started racing with possibilities.

Drug offenses? Burglary? Assault? Was he a former Russian spy or something? With that phony Texan accent he threw at me, I'd say he was a pretty bad one. This definitely made sense. He *did* have something to do with Victory Cup Valentino's disappearance! I knew it! I knew it all along. Case closed for the great Piper Sandstone.

"So, it says here, a record of...forging checks?"

Forging checks?

"Wait, what? What else?"

"Um...that's it," Morgan says, his eyes moving around the screen like pinballs, desperate to find some dirt like I was. "There's nothing else?"

"Check fraud. You've got to be kidding me."

"I wish I was. This was in the early 2000s. Apparently, he did it for years. Got unlucky once and got caught. He paid a huge amount in restitution and did a few years in the slammer. When he got out, it looks like he stayed clean."

Why did he do it? Was he young and desperate? Needed

to pay the rent somehow? Or is there something more lurking under the surface?

A deep sigh. "Well, looks like a dead end."

"Sorry," Morgan said, looking as disappointed as I felt.

"Dude, it's not your fault he's not some former Russian spy or something. That's what I was hoping for anyway."

"Guess not," he chuckled. "What are you gonna do next?"

"Hmm...the Delta Queens mentioned that Susan has an aunt in Montgomery. Aunt Mary or something? If I'm not getting anything from Adam Kane, then I guess I'll have to look somewhere else. Maybe she knows the whereabouts of her niece."

Where are you, Susan? What are you up to?

"It's a lead. It's not much, but it's something. Probably worth checking out."

7

SURPRISE VISIT

In Montgomery, Alabama, past the red-bricked steeple church, stood the Butternut Bakehouse, a small bakery with its door propped open so the scent of fresh bread would flood out onto the street, warm and sweet and so mouth-watering that I almost forgot what I came here for.

Through the glass window, I could see a plump woman behind the counter, kneading dough like her life depended on it. She has long silvery hair pulled up in a bun, and her cheeks were streaked with flour. Mary Tate, I guessed. Susan's, the dog trainer's aunt.

"Well, howdy there! C'mon on inside, why don't ya," she called out to me when she spotted me standing outside. Her eyes crinkled when she smiled.

"Hi there. I'm Detective Piper Sandstone."

"Detective?"

"Yes, Chicago PD," I say, flashing her my badge. The smile in her eyes evaporated like a dark rolling fog.

"Oh. Well, I'm guessing you ain't here for my famous old-fashioned cinnamon rolls."

"Afraid not. But it smells amazing. I'll have to try it some-time," I offered pathetically. She wiped her hands on her well-worn apron and heaved a sigh.

"Is it my Suzie?"

I thought about making something up, saving her the trouble. But the forlorn look on her face told me I shouldn't.

"Yes. Susan Tate."

"Ah, well. I've heard the rumors, you know. The accusa-tions. Stealing a dog. How preposterous! My Suzie could never," Mary said, so affronted that her round cheeks rattled as she talked. It was easy to tell that she absolutely adored her niece and looked after her with a fierce protectiveness.

"So, she never came upstate?"

"No! She never made it. She texted me that day. That day of the 'dog-nap' or whatever slickerin' owl charades that was," she offered, putting her fingers up in air quotes. "She was supposed to come to visit."

"And she texted you that she couldn't make it?"

"Oh no. She texted me saying she was on her way."

She did? How was this never mentioned before? Well, this changed everything, didn't it?

"So, when she never showed up, of course, I got worried," Mary continued, wringing her flour-stained hands together. "I called Valorie Channing because I wanted to talk to my Suzie."

"And what did she say?"

Mary hung her head and then looked at the ceiling, trying to ward off tears. I stood there awkwardly as she composed herself.

"They said my Suzie had disappeared. Valorie said she won a lottery of some kind and had traveled out of the country."

A lottery? Well, well, well. Things just got interesting.

"I just...I just don't understand. She would have told me. She tells me everything!"

That's true. It didn't seem like Susan was the type to just up and leave. She was definitely close with her aunt. Susan would have told her.

Someone was downright lying, and my intuition said it wasn't sweet Mary Tate.

"It's just her and me, you know? Since her mama died. She's my Suzie," Mary whispered, tears dripping down her cheeks slowly.

Had Susan Tate been kidnapped as well? Was she with Victory?

"You think something happened to her, don't you?" Mary asked, her voice starting to break.

I gave no answer.

"You'll bring her back, won't you?"

Again, I gave no answer.

8

YOU TELL ME

Apparently, dogs had to eat three times a day too. And not just my leftover scraps, it turned out. They needed actual food and everything. Huh. Who knew?

The Fuzzy Wuzzy Furball Pet Store was the only pet shop in town. Even from outside, it looked stuffed to the gills with pet toys and cages and about a hundred other weird contraptions. I'd actually love to meet the person who came up with that ridiculous name.

As I pushed through the door, I was greeted by a bored-looking woman in an apron. With her deep scowl, I guessed she was *not* the one who spent a good chunk of time thinking up that name.

"Welcome to the Fuzzy Wuzzy Furball Pet Store," she seemed to force out in a droning, monotonous voice. "My name's Angie. What can I help you with?"

"Hi, yes. I need food. For my dog."

We stared at each other for a beat. She waited for me to add something else. And then sighed in annoyance when she realized I didn't have a clue what in God's green earth I was doing.

"Alrighty then. What kind of dog do you have?"

"Erm. Does it matter?"

Another sigh. "Yes. We have dry food and canned food. Specialized dog food for small breeds like chihuahuas. We've got a whole 'nother thing for puppies. And then there are adult dogs, too. And big dogs and what have you," she recited, her eyes glazing over.

"Oh. I don't really...know...."

Her eyes bore into me as I stuttered, getting more and more annoyed by the second.

"Oh! I have a picture! I have a picture of him."

I whipped out my loaner phone, an ancient iPhone 5SE that sweet Margie so kindly gave me when she learned I moved to town without one. There on the lock screen was Mister, head tilted down and huge brown eyes looking up at my camera. That damn dog. Making me take pictures and buy all kinds of stuff for him. It was those damn floppy ears. How could floppy ears be so cute?

"That's a beagle lab mix. I'm guessing five months old?"

"Sounds about right. He just...showed up. At my house."

She handed me a few small tubs of fancy-looking dog food.

"That's got tender turkey, green beans, and sweet potatoes in gravy. It's got protein, vitamins, minerals. A completely balanced meal for your growing dog. Specially formulated for medium to large breeds."

Would you look at that? The damn dog would be eating better than me!

"Well, then. Guess that's settled. I'll take maybe a couple more packs of those."

She ran her eyes over me, giving me a thorough scan like it was the first time she was seeing me.

"I'm guessin' you need supplies too?"

I walked out of the Fuzzy Wuzzy Furball Pet Store juggling three paper bags filled with...stuff. Food and treats and rawhide bones and dental sticks and dog shampoo. And I thought dogs were low maintenance. Ha!

I made my way over to cross the street when the sudden blaring of a car horn made me jump. The dog supplies flew into the air as I leaped away from the car that was a hair strand away from ramming right into me.

"Oy! Watch it, lady!" yelled the driver from his open window. He was pimply faced with a wispy mustache. He looked young, painfully young. Maybe sixteen or so. Loud rap music was blasting from his stereo.

"Hey! You watch it!"

He parked the car and stepped out of the sleek silver BMW, looking smaller outside the confines of the vehicle.

"What's the matter with you? You almost ran into me!"

"You were in my way," he stated simply. He strode toward the pet store, not giving me a second glance. He was wearing a suit a few sizes too big for him and a tie haphazardly knotted together.

"Who the hell gave you your license?" I managed to yell out. But he was already inside the store, and I was surrounded by the recently purchased dog paraphernalia scattered along the sidewalk.

My gaze fell back on the car, now resting a few feet from my thighs. A silver BMW X3. 2019 model, at the latest. What a pompous ass, even if he was only a kid.

On second thought, how could a teenager afford a car like that? Hmm, interesting.

Maybe I should ask the Delta Queens about this kid.

9

BEACH ATTRACTIONS

"I just don't see the point, is all," huffed Rosemary. "It's a ridiculous thing to do."

"Ridiculous? It's a life-saving skill!" Doris retorted, slathering sunscreen on her face. She had on a short wetsuit that made it look like she was going surfing and a huge straw hat that could almost pass for an umbrella.

"Everyone has to swim at some point in their lives, Rosie," Patty Sue chimed in. She wore a vintage-looking high-waisted two-piece set that made her look decades younger. "Anyone see where I put my shades?"

"They're on your head, sweetie," replied Rosemary quickly before going back to her tirade on beaches. "Well, I've gone on 60-plus years without it. A shark could chomp off my foot! Or...or...heaven forbid, an octopus could strangle me half to death!"

"Oh honey, it's that little string bikini you have on that's going to strangle you to death," Doris piped in without missing a beat. I couldn't help but let out a snort of laughter.

Because what Rosemary had on was definitely...little. She

dazzled in a flimsy bikini top and ruffled shorts on her bottom. If I could ask for anything in my life, it would be to have Rosemary's confidence.

"Ah yes. Let's see if I can catch any fish with these things if you know what I mean," Rosemary quipped with a wink, adjusting her bikini to show more skin.

"Well, how will you catch anything if you refuse to go in the water?" sighed Doris.

"Oh, just dip your toes in the water, Rosie. It's all good fun," Margie urged. She was in a more conservative mint-colored one-piece with a sarong tied around her waist.

"Fine, fine," Rosemary gave up. "But if a sea monster pulls me down to the depths of the ocean floor, I'll be haunting all of you. Except you, Sharon, sweetheart. I know you have nothing to do with this."

That was partly true. The trip to the beach was originally Patty Sue's idea, seconded by Doris and Margie.

"We need a break from all the dognappings and mysteries around here," announced Patty Sue a few weeks ago at the Crabby Clam café. Nothing was going on with the case, and we were bleeding our brains dry thinking about it.

"Oh! A beach trip!" exclaimed Margie. "That would be just delightful!"

"Orange Beach would be perfect! We haven't been there in ages!" Doris said, her eyes sparkling underneath her spectacles.

"Noooo, not the beach," groaned Rosemary. But before the day had ended, plans were already made, and all Rosemary could do was sulk about it.

But I did agree to drive them here, so I guess I was partly responsible. Much to Rosemary's chagrin.

Still, I was glad I agreed. Orange Beach was only an hour

and a half drive from Savory, but it felt like I just traveled to the Caribbean, what with its fine white sand and majestic turquoise waters. The sun was fierce today, but a cool, salty breeze in the air made the muggy heat bearable.

"Let's go, Rosie. You're not getting out of this," Doris ordered, pulling Rosemary into the gentle, lapping waves of the ocean.

"It's freezing! It's freezing!" Rosemary yelped, running from the surf.

"What are you talking about? It's the perfect temperature!" giggled Margie, who was already knee-deep in the water and splashing around merrily.

"C'mon, Rosie. I'll teach you how to swim," I told Rosemary as she gripped my arm so tight, her knuckles turned white.

"You most definitely will *not*," she said in her most indignant voice. And then, "Eeeeeek, it's an octopus! An octopus has got my leg!" Rosemary jumped around frantically, screeching and flailing her arms around.

"It's seaweed, you dum-dum," Doris hollered, grabbing the damp, green plants swirling around Rosemary's leg and throwing it at her.

"Oh, good Lord in heaven. Why do those things have to twirl around your foot like that? Let's just go. I told you this was a bad idea. It's not...."

Rosemary trailed off, never finishing her sentence. Her jaw dropped open as she caught sight of something in the distance. I followed her gaze and saw...

Men. Throngs of young, tanned, muscular men in skimpy beach shorts jumping into the water. There must have been a dozen of them. Maybe college kids on summer break?

"Oh me-oh-my," Rosemary said airily, her voice suddenly different from just a few seconds ago.

"Alright, keep it in your pants, Rosie," Doris snapped with a roll of her eyes, already knowing where this was going.

"Whoa. Even I wouldn't mind rubbing a little sunscreen on those bodies," murmured Patty Sue, looking on appreciatively.

"I second that motion. Third it, fourth it, fifth it," Rosemary added, still looking and nodding. Her face was dead serious like she was appraising artwork.

"Oh, good grief," I heard Doris say.

"Mornin', ladies," called one of the guys as he treaded water near us. He was a dark-haired twenty-something with an impressive six-pack. Oh wait, was that an eight-pack? How was that even possible?

"Hi there! Mornin'!" Rosemary replied with a flirty wave. The guy ran past us, then dove in and swam away. Rosemary stood frozen in awe like she had just seen a mermaid.

Well," she started, turning to Doris with an almost indignant look. "Why didn't you bring me to the beach sooner?"

10

VALORIE CHANNING

For all its pomp and circumstance, I'd never actually been to the Channing mansion before. Not this close, at least. They lived in a breathtaking southern Victorian estate sitting on twenty acres of lush green land. I rolled in leisurely through a private cobblestone road until I reached an iron gate.

Once inside, I came face to face with a spectacular estate that looked like it belonged on the cover of *Southern Living* magazine. The property was dotted with majestic Weeping Willows and Magnolia trees that beckoned me down its long drive way.

I parked and walked to the front door, a huge double wooden door with antique brass knockers in the shape of lion's heads on each side. I lifted one giant brass knocker and gave two knocks.

I waited for a few long minutes, worried that no one was home. But then, one of the doors cracked open just enough for me to see a woman's face staring at me.

"Yes?" asked a timid young woman in a black and white maid's outfit. "Who are you?"

"Hi, I'm Sharon. Sharon Sanders. I'm here to see Mrs. Channing. Is she in?"

She looked at me confused, wary of letting in a literal stranger, which was understandable. So, I put on the brightest smile I could muster.

"Oh, I'm new in town, and I heard about what happened with Victory. It must be devastating! How's she holding up with her missing poodle? I know that the Westminster Dog show is only a week away, and I can't begin to imagine how stressful this has been."

If I wanted to get close to Valorie Channing, I knew I had to play my cards right. Hit her where it hurts. Play the concerned, consoling neighbor.

"Oh," said the maid. The worry left her face, and she started jabbering like she'd decided that she could trust me. "She is devastated. Been a little harsh on the sheriff lately, but I think he understands," she explained. "Come on in. I'm sure Valorie wouldn't mind some company."

"Who wouldn't mind some company?" came a booming voice from behind her. The tall figure of Valorie Channing stood with one hand on her hip. With her white silken pantsuit and her golden blonde hair pulled up in loose tendrils on her head, she looked like a Greek goddess in her palace.

Her eyes roamed up and down me, scoping me out.

"And who are you?" Her pale gray eyes seemed to pierce me where I stood.

"Oh, I'm Shar—," I started.

"You're the girl from the restaurant," she stated, cutting me off. "I recognize you."

"Yes, at the Crabby Clam Café. I'm new here, and I heard about your dog," I added, putting on a slightly pouty face. "I own a dog too. At least, I used to."

I noticed her eyes had softened slightly, so I went in for the kill.

"I just came to see how you were holding up," I continued. "I can't imagine how you must be feeling."

"Yes, well...it's been..." she uttered with a sigh, like talking about it was just so exhausting.

"Well, come on in then," she said finally, waving her arm inside. I tried not to gawk as I entered the house. The front parlor by itself was as big as my whole apartment back in Chicago, with glittering diamond-shaped crystals hanging from the chandeliers and dark mahogany paneled walls.

I followed her inside, careful not to gape too openly at the sheer luxury. Everything was gold and silver and glittering. The rich, earthy scent of incense diffused through the air. It did not feel like the Savory I know. It felt like a city inside of a city.

"What breed was your dog?" she asked me as she gracefully sat down on her sofa. I sat as well—without the grace—nearly sinking in the soft cushions.

"A German Shepherd. Her name was Missy," I replied. I had never owned a dog in my life. Except for Mister, of course. But she didn't need to know that.

"Hmm, a big dog."

"She acted small, though. She was quite a sissy for a German Shepherd," I explained, and Valorie laughed, loud and piercing.

"I've heard a lot of folks say they don't think the dog show would go on without Victory," I added.

She leaned back in her seat, looking suddenly bored by my sudden segue of our conversation.

"Bah! It will go on as planned. No one really cares about a dog," she stated with alarming indifference.

Really? I wanted to say. The whole town was looking for this dog! If this was her poker face, then it was pretty good. Wasn't she supposed to be grieving?

"And the sheriff isn't doing his job at all! They're useless, I'm telling you," she continued.

"He said folks saw the dog trainer with Victory. Thought maybe she stole it," I prompted, as casually as I could.

"Oh please, I saw her myself. On the CCTV cameras, skittering around with the dog. Running away or God knows what." Valorie paused, waving her hand around like she was craving a cigarette. "And Jake better do his job right! Actually look for her instead of asking these inane questions. Useless, the whole lot of them," she snapped with annoyance.

"Maybe you should hire an investigator or—"

"No, I won't," she said quickly. "My husband doesn't fancy the idea, so I won't."

Then who is Adam Kane, and why are you sneaking off to secret meetings with him? I wondered.

"So, where is Susan anyway?"

"I have no clue." She leaned back on the sofa, exasperated.

"Jake said she won a lottery or something." I threw this out to see if she would take the bait.

"Jake said that?" she said, sitting up properly now. Her eyes focused on me, like a hawk zeroing in on its prey.

"No, I—"

Her eyes narrowed, glaring and seething like a gray storm. For a few seconds, we just sat there staring at each other.

"Please leave, Candice. Or whatever it is you call yourself," she spat coldly, shooing me away like a stray dog.

There was something else in her eyes besides blatant annoyance. Something that looked vaguely like suspicion. Was she suspicious of me? Or was she hiding something? It was hard to tell.

Before I knew it, she was up on her feet. I knew I could push no further. But at least I still got something helpful. I knew Susan didn't win the lottery as Valorie had told Mary Tate, and I knew she most definitely did not go to Montgomery.

"I'm sorry for pushing. Truly, I apologize. I didn't mean to offend you," I said, placating her.

Her eyes softened again, although I sensed she still wanted to kick me out. But I couldn't leave. Not yet. I had a plan, and I needed a few more minutes inside the Channing mansion.

"Hm. I suppose...I suppose I'm sorry too. It's been a hard couple of weeks," she said, a trace of sadness in her eyes.

"No need to apologize. I can't begin to imagine what you've been through. And I've wasted enough of your time, so I'll get out of your hair. It's just...um...."

"What? What is it?"

"Can I use your bathroom?" I asked with a pretend grimace. "I'm terribly sorry. I had a large iced coffee before I got here." I lied.

Annoyance flashed across her face again, and she rolled her eyes at me.

"Fine. The bathroom is right over there, just through the kitchen," she pointed before sashaying out of the living room.

"Thank you so much!" I called after her. "I'll just use your bathroom and then skedaddle right on out of here."

She didn't bother replying to me, so I hurried into the kitchen, surveying the room. Luckily, the place was empty. No wait staff or hired chefs loitering about.

The kitchen was as grand as the rest of the house though it looked much newer. There was another gorgeous chandelier hovering above a beautiful dinette. The granite countertops were so clean and shiny, I could see my reflection in them. I marveled over the sleek stainless steel appliances that looked like they had never been touched.

Oh, right. The bug! I had to plant the surveillance bug!

I took out the tiny RF bug I had in my pocket. It was small, the size of a dime. I pulled out a strip of good old duct tape I had wrapped around a pen cap and stuck the bug under the kitchen island countertop.

That should do. Just in time, too, because I heard footsteps from the hallway coming to the kitchen.

"You find everything alright?" the maid asked.

"Yes, thank you for letting me use the bathroom. My bladder was about to explode," I responded with a forced laugh.

Luckily, she didn't think anything was amiss and chortled along with me.

"Well, let me get out of your way now. Thank you for everything."

"Of course. Come again soon," she said, although she probably only meant it as pleasantries.

Trust me, I won't have to, I thought to myself as I headed out to my car. I got in and slowly backed out of the estate. Once I was clear of the giant iron gates, I allowed myself a devilish smile.

11

BUGGED AND BITTER

"What are we listening for again?" asked Patty Sue.

"Well, anything really. Anything important," said Margie. We were at her house, all huddled around the recording device hooked up to the surveillance bug I had placed in the Channing's kitchen. It had been a few days, and still no bite, just the grating sounds of the blender when the maids made Valorie's morning smoothie.

"Lord, this is boring," huffed Rosemary for about the fifteenth time. "I was expecting something juicy and exciting, ya know?"

"Shush! We're not the Dentures and Diamonds Crime Squad for nothing!" admonished Doris. "It might take a while. And that's fine. We got all the time in the world, ladies." She sprawled out on the sofa, slowly sipping her Earl Grey tea.

"We just need some sort of evidence. I have a feeling Valorie's hiding something. Something big," I said, taking my place on the sofa.

We sat there for what felt like hours, listening to the

crackles of static from the bug's radio frequency. Since it was a Sunday, the Crabby Clam Café was closed, so I geared myself for an all-day, all-night listening session. I stared at the little machine, at its recording tapes rolling around the gears.

C'mon, Valorie. Give us something good.

"Boring, boring, boring," sighed Rosemary. "I'll get us something to eat. Watching paint dry is more fun than this."

...what do you mean?

A voice emanated from the machine, crackling and snapping to life all of a sudden. All five heads in the living room whipped toward the sound being picked up by the bug.

A voice. A male voice.

"Wait, what? Who was that?" Rosemary posed, backtracking toward us.

"I don't know. But he sounds familiar." I'd definitely heard that voice before.

*...we have to follow through...*the same male voice said between the sounds of ice clinking in a glass.

...I know. I know what we talked about. I just need more time.

This from another voice—a female. Airy and soft-spoken but with a tinge of hardness.

Valorie.

...not part of the plan... the male voice again, sounding agitated.

That voice, that accent, that familiar twang. Where had I heard it before?

Then it came to me, the man from the café. A man with a fake Texan accent. Him reverting to his natural voice when I called him out.

"Oh my gosh, that's Adam Kane!"

"You're right! Yes, that's him!" exclaimed Doris. "I've talked to him a few times too!"

...look, just calm down, okay? Valorie said. I heard sounds of liquid pouring into a glass, and I imagined Valorie bringing Adam a drink and rubbing his back, trying to soothe him.

...don't tell me to calm down! We have to follow through with the plan... Adam snarled.

What plan? What are you two up to? Or better yet, what did you already do?

...we will, alright? Valorie promised and then added *...we'll do everything we talked about....*

And then their voices faded out as they left the kitchen. The ladies and I sat frozen in our seats, staring at each other for a minute before Rosemary broke the silence.

"I take it back!" Rosemary announced with a giant grin. "None of this is boring!"

12

SECRET AGENDA

"Two cappuccinos. Got it."

And table two ordered the red beans and rice special. Table five wanted a tall, half-caf soy latte at 120 degrees. Exactly 120 degrees! Who orders these things, I thought. Will they have a conniption if it's one degree higher or lower than 120? And table six ordered a...

"Sharon, honey. Could I get one of those croissants? They're absolutely delightful," drawls Madeline, one of the Crabby Clam's snootiest customers. Today, she was wearing some sort of Chanel three-piece suit. In this humid heat, I didn't know how she hadn't passed out from heatstroke yet.

"One croissant. On the way."

"Oh no, honey. It's 'kwa-sah,' not 'kroi-sant,'" she said, looking at me like I just stomped on her foot. She turned to her equally snooty friends and gave a little condescending chuckle. "These Americans. Just butchering the French language."

"You're from Denver," I muttered under my breath, subtly rolling my eyes.

"What was that?"

"Oh, nothing. Just one *kwa-sah* coming right up."

Sigh. Just another busy afternoon at the Crabby Clam Café. It was Saturday, so pretty much everyone had descended upon the café to have lunch, relax, and make the most of their weekend. Exactly when Carla, my coworker, had decided to go MIA.

The small café was buzzing, voices and laughter bouncing around the red-brick walls. On the far end, at their usual table, sat the Delta Queens, sipping at their teas and munching on scones. I decided to stop by their table because I was never too busy for a little chat with them.

"Can I get you ladies anything?"

"Oh, no, Sharon. We're good," said Margie shyly. Even if she wanted anything, she sometimes wouldn't even tell me.

"You're such a sweetheart for asking. But you go on ahead. You're busier than a cat on a hot tin roof up in here! This place is packed!" exclaimed Doris.

"Speaking of hot," Rosemary piped in. She nodded her head toward the door which had just opened, the bell above making a loud ringing sound.

Jake strolled in.

He was in casual clothes today, a sleeveless red flannel button-down and dark jeans. There was a hint of stubble on his face, making him look even more rugged than usual.

"That man is finer than a frog hair split four ways," said Rosemary, roving her eyes up and down Jake's form.

"Oh, cool it, Rosemary," Doris quipped. "You go on ahead, Sharon dear. We're still finishing up these lovely scones."

"Yes, ma'am."

"Ooooh, he's looking at you all lovey-dovey. I'm telling you right now, ask him out on a date!" Rosemary practically begged. Her voice was so loud that I'm pretty sure dogs a mile away heard that.

"Oh shush, Rosemary. You're embarrassing us all," Patty Sue scolded.

Jake sat at the far end of the café and stared at me with an intense look on his face. Then his expression morphed into a soft, shy smile as I walked over to take his order.

"Why hello there, Sheriff."

"Sharon. Nice to see you again," he said, so formal. But he was still smiling like a little kid.

"What can I get for you?"

"I'll take your red beans and rice special. It's my favorite."

"Ah, yes. The ol' beans and rice. It's everyone's favorite. We've had a couple dozen lunch orders already today. Can't blame them, though. It's pretty amazing."

"How do you guys make it? It's so rich and full of flavor."

"Ah, Sheriff. I'm not in the business to divulge any Crabby Clam secrets," I tutted at him, pretending like I actually knew. The truth was, I had no clue. But he was right. The red beans and rice were to die for. Thick and creamy with lots of andouille sausage for that perfect smoky flavor. The thought of it made my stomach rumble.

"Great choice though. I'll be right back with your order."

I must have taken two steps away from him when my shoe landed on a small puddle on the floor.

Great, somebody spilled their drink.

As I gingerly stepped to the side, my other foot met another puddle. With a squeak of my shoe, I felt myself gliding and slipping off balance.

It was all in slow motion, the way my arms flailed in the

air and my legs twisted into some sort of pretzel. I braced myself for a painful thwack on the tile, for a bruised head and a bad concussion.

But it never came.

Instead, I landed in a pair of strong arms. When I opened my eyes, I saw Jake staring down at me, an impish smile on his face.

"Careful there. We can't have you hitting your pretty head now, can we?"

"Can't bring you your food if I did."

With a quick lift of his arms, I was on my feet again.

"Thanks, Sheriff."

"Don't worry about it." He sat back down on his chair, studying me. Like he wanted to say something else.

"Need anything else?"

"No, no," he said, his eyes cool and calculating. Trained right at me. "I was just wondering if you'd like to go out with me sometime? Like on a friendly date?"

Oh. Great. That.

"Only if you want to, of course," he added casually.

I was considering how I could politely let him down. Even a friendly date wasn't my cup of tea right now. From the corner of my eye, I saw Rosemary and the Delta Queens looking on proudly and giving me giddy thumbs-up signs like they knew exactly what we were talking about even though they were on the opposite side of the café.

Then a sudden thought occurred to me. Wait! This was good. If I said yes, then perhaps I could get more intel about the case.

What? Are you seriously going to use him like that? This second thought seemed to come from the opposite side of my brain.

"Yes," I said, interrupting my internal babble.

"Yeah?" he asked, just as surprised with my answer as I was. His calculating eyes were replaced with bright, hopeful ones.

"Sure. That would be great. Just tell me when."

Our bubble was burst when snooty Chanel suit lady started snapping her fingers at me and asking for her *kwa-sah.*

"Well, duty calls. I'll see you around, Sheriff."

"Here's your red beans and rice," I said, placing a steaming hot bowl in front of the man sitting at the counter before I realized my mistake. "I'm sorry, this isn't your order."

"Nope, just coffee for me today. Thanks," he replied with a smile.

"Sorry, it's been a long day already," I said before turning around to the table behind him. "I believe this order belongs to you, sir." My embarrassment was trumped by my curiosity, so I headed over to the ladies' table.

"Who is that?" I nodded subtly at the well-dressed older gentleman sipping coffee and reading a newspaper at the restaurant counter.

"Oh, that's Raymond Price," said Patty Sue, almost absent-mindedly. She was twirling her tea with a spoon to dissolve the sugar cubes.

"Richard Price, dear," Doris said kindly.

"Oh yes, yes. Richard. Oh, I remember him! From my old partying days."

"Partying?" I asked. Sure, Patty Sue seemed a bit eccentric, but she didn't seem like a hard-partying type of girl. Nor did this Richard Price character with his shiny silver hair, looking dashing against his dark blue blazer.

"Not the kind of partying you're thinking of, dear," Doris said to me, chuckling slightly. "More like high-society events. Our Patty Sue here is quite connected with the social circles. Richard is one of the nouveau riche that worked his way up from poverty," Doris whispered.

"Pfft. He can come party with me any day if you catch my drift," said Rosemary, shimmying her shoulders and giving me a not-so-subtle wink. "Such a silver fox, that man. Rawr!"

I giggled at Rosemary's enthusiasm though I could see why she was attracted to him. Richard Price seemed fit as a fiddle for a man I guessed was in his early 60s. He had quite the air of sophistication about him with his sport coat, jeans, loafers, and that gorgeous head of hair.

"Oh, I hardly think he has time to party anymore, Rosie," Margie said innocently. "He's quite occupied with running his business."

"I know that, Margie, but all work and no play makes Richard a dull boy," Rosemary countered, rolling her eyes. Then she looked at me and explained. "Richard Price owns a chain of banks here in town. He's business partners with Mr. Channing."

"They're quite chummy, those two," Doris hummed as she looked through the Crabby Clam's menu as if she hadn't memorized the whole thing already. "I think we should have another one of those lovely scones. What do you think, ladies? Share one with me?"

As the ladies argued about what flavor scone to get, my gaze fell back on Mr. Richard Price. He drained the last of his coffee and folded up the newspaper. Then he strolled out of the café and got into a sleek silver BMW that matched his stylish hair.

13

DEADLIEST DATE

"Well, well, well. Look at you. You clean up nicely," Jake remarked with a satisfied smirk.

We agreed to meet up at the Crabby Clam, a sort of neutral territory, for our "friendly" date. I was wearing an off-the-shoulder white blouse and jeans, ones that didn't have rips in them. Nancy probably stuffed those into my suitcase for this exact occasion. I didn't bother with my hair or makeup because the humidity would have ruined it anyway. And I couldn't put on makeup to save my life.

"What, you didn't recognize me without my Crabby Clam Café t-shirt?" I volleyed back with my own smirk. Then I noticed that Jake did indeed clean up nicely. In a sport coat and jeans with his rugged stubble, he looked like a model on one of those Abercrombie catalogs.

"So, where are we going? You never mentioned," I asked as we stepped into his Silverado truck. Surprises typically made me feel anxious, but I was, after all, a woman on a mission. In the confines of the vehicle, though, I could smell Jake's spicy, cinnamon scent. It was quite distracting.

"Well, seeing as you're new around these parts, I figured I'd take you to the second-best seafood restaurant in all of Savory, Alabama. You like seafood, right?"

"No, I hate it," I teased.

From afar, The Red Claw restaurant looked like it was just a little shack near the ocean. The water was peaceful and calm as the late afternoon sun glistened and reflected on it, like something from a painting. The wooden pier jutted way out into the water, and along both sides were boats of every size and shape, from ragged little dinghies to shiny white deck boats.

The place looked packed, and as we pulled in, I saw tables and chairs filled with customers digging into plates of steaming seafood.

Inside, chefs bustled around the kitchen, and workers carried in large coolers filled with freshly caught fish and oysters, the day's catch.

"Everything here is really fresh. Pretty much straight out of the water, you know?" said Jake, with excitement in his voice.

"I can imagine. They've got the perfect location right here on the pier."

We ordered the seafood au gratin, a rich, creamy casserole with baked haddock and sea scallops topped with the most amazing molten cheese. Jake and I were quiet for a while, focused on our food.

"So," I finally said, trying to sound as casual as I could. "How's the case going?"

"Oh, you know," he said between mouthfuls. "Nothing the public doesn't already know. Prize-winning dog is missing. There's CCTV footage of the dog trainer leaving the premises, looking over her shoulder, running away. Now she's disappeared."

"You think she did it?" It was a long shot for me to ask the town sheriff, but I figured I might as well.

He smiled at me, but his eyes looked serious. "You know I can't answer that."

"No, no, of course. Sorry, it's just...crazy. Crazy that something like this could happen here." And here I thought Savory, Alabama was nothing more than a sleepy little town.

"Definitely. This is one of the most perplexing cases I've ever had as sheriff."

"And how long have you been the sheriff?"

"Almost five years now." He sighed, rubbing at his stubbled chin. "I just wish Victory and Susan would just show up, you know. Safe and sound. So, this craziness would be over."

Jake seemed like he was about to say something more when his phone started ringing in his pocket. He answered in a hurry, excusing himself from the table.

It couldn't have been more than a few minutes later when he came back with a frazzled look I had never seen on him before.

"What's wrong?"

"There was a body found in the Tombigbee River," he said, his voice eerily calm. But his eyes were as wide as our dinner plates now.

"What!"

"I'm really sorry about this, Sharon. I'm afraid we'll have to cut our dinner short. I have to go." He reached for his wallet and called for the check.

There was a sudden sinking feeling in my chest. And not because of the date that had been cut short. So much for a sleepy little town. I had to think quick.

"I'll go with you."

Jake stopped in his tracks, fingers digging into his wallet. "No, you most definitely will not."

"Why not?"

"One, you're a civilian. Two, I don't think you should see something like this."

"Why not?" I challenged him. "Because I'm a woman, you think I can't handle it?"

Suddenly, I thought back to that crime scene photo I saw of the murdered drug dealer. Blood splattered on the walls, the written warning. That seemed like ages ago, but I still felt as nauseous now as I did then. Keep it together, Piper!

"I didn't say that," Jake said, heaving a sigh.

"Well, you didn't have to. Besides, I don't have a ride back to town," I said, raising my eyebrows in desperation. An obstacle I was hoping he wouldn't have time to figure out.

Another sigh. He was pretty exasperated with me already. "You're quite annoying, aren't you?" He smiled as he said this, which meant I hadn't pushed my luck. Yet.

"That's my middle name."

"Sharon Annoying Sanders. Fits perfectly. C'mon, let's go, but you're staying in the truck."

"Yes, of course," I agreed, climbing into the vehicle before he did. He looked at me through the window, smiling and shaking his head. "Well? Let's go, slowpoke!"

Luckily, the Tombigbee River wasn't too far from the pier. When we arrived, there were two police cars already there and the county coroner. The deputy and several cops were securing the scene.

"Stay inside the truck, Sharon," Jake said sternly like I would bolt as soon as the vehicle rolled to a stop. Which is exactly what I wanted to do, of course. But I put my hands up and showed him my most innocent face.

"I know, I know. I'll stay inside the truck."

"Don't move. I'll be right back," Jake said as he stepped out of the car. Then he locked the door from outside with his key, which was more of a ceremonial gesture than anything because I could still unlock the door from inside.

Five minutes. I lasted five minutes before I clicked on the lock and slowly opened the door. The humid air hit my face immediately, and I felt a swarm of mosquitoes descending on my skin. I wanted to walk toward the edge of the river where the officers were congregating, but I knew Jake wouldn't let me near the scene. From where we were parked, I figured I could grab a peek if I got a little higher up. Maybe I could climb a tree?

But then, a better thought occurred to me. I decided to use the hood of the truck for leverage instead. I clambered up quickly, trying not to mess up Jake's shiny black Chevy. From this vantage point, I was able to see over the crowd. I pulled Margie's loaner phone from my pocket and used the camera feature to zoom in on the scene.

That's when I saw it, grainy on my phone but still clear as day. A woman's body, pale green and bloated beyond recognition. Seaweed twirled around her mud-caked legs. There was a rope tied to her waist. She was never meant to be found.

I recognized the baby blue summer dress she was wearing from the news clip of the CCTV footage. The lock of shiny brown hair. The pile of braided bracelets on her right arm.

There was no question—it was definitely Susan Tate.

14

VENOM

It was already way past midnight, but every nerve in my body was still vibrating with nervous energy over the discovery at the Tombigbee River. There was no way I was just hauling myself off to bed. Not when they had just found Susan Tate's body.

And that's precisely why I found myself tip-toeing into the Channing estate well after dark, abandoning my car a few blocks away. My plan was to sneak over to Susan's place to see if I could find any clues.

The cottage had been blocked off for the investigation once the cops changed the case to a homicide after discovering Susan's body. There was bright yellow barrier tape surrounding the property, practically zig-zagging on all sides and corners.

But not enough to stop me.

All I had to do was sneak onto the Channing property and crawl across the lawn to avoid the security cameras until I reached the cottage. Then I stepped over the tape, put on a pair of gloves, and picked the lock on the door. And just like that, I was in. Easy as pie.

It wasn't my intention to steal anything or tamper with evidence. I just wanted to...know what happened. I wanted to gather more information. I knew Susan Tate held the key to the mystery. I could feel it. I wasn't quite sure what to look for, but there was no harm in snooping around.

Susan Tate's little cottage on the south end of the estate was cozy and cute, with vintage-looking furniture and eclectic artwork plastered on the walls. I pointed my flashlight at one of the abstract paintings and found a small "Susan Tate" signature on the bottom.

So, she was an artist too. A woman of many talents. From what the ladies had told me about her, Susan seemed well-adjusted, happy with her life in Savory and her life with the Channings. Happy with her job, with Victory. Which begged the question: Why did you run away? Were you trying to hide? What happened to you, Susan Tate?

Nothing seemed off about the living room. Nothing out of place. Susan kept a clean house. There were a few magazines strewn around and an empty glass on the end table, but that was pretty much it.

I moved into the bedroom, the bright light on my phone illuminating the wooden floors. A quick sweep of the room revealed nothing unusual, except...wait.

Was that a suitcase?

There, tucked beside the bed, was a black rolling suitcase the size of a carry-on. The zippers were nearly bursting at the seams. It was stuffed and ready to go. Susan Tate was going somewhere. But where? And why didn't she take the packed suitcase?

None of this made sense. Why were you running away? What did you do?

I tip-toed out of the room and into the kitchen. Moonlight was streaming through the window above the sink, so I turned off the flashlight on my phone. Like the rest of the cottage, everything had been put away. There wasn't even a stray plate in the sink.

I opened drawers and cabinets, hoping to find...something. Again, I didn't know what I was looking for. I felt like a kid again, clawing at my cereal box for the mystery prize.

Inside one of the small drawers on the far end of the countertop, I saw a small notepad opened in the middle. Curiously, I examined it closer. On the page, I saw a haphazardly scrawled note that sent a chill down my spine.

I'm sorry I don't have time to explain, but don't go golfing...

And that was all that was written. It ended abruptly in the middle of a sentence. Don't go golfing? With whom? Who's this message for? I assume this is Susan's handwriting. And it looked like she was in a hurry when she wrote this the way the pen mark ran across the notepad. And why do I get the feeling there was more she wanted to write?

"Freeze!"

A voice boomed from behind and made me jump up with a yelp. I turned around and saw a figure emerging from the shadows.

"Oh my God! Jake!"

He was still in the clothes he was wearing from our date

that was cut short. His eyes went wide as dinner plates when he registered who the intruder was.

"Sharon?"

"What are you doing here?"

"What am I doing here? What are you doing here?"

"You're supposed to be at the station," I said, putting my hands up reflexively. I didn't know why I said that. *Way to dig your grave, Piper.*

Something in his eyes snapped. He dropped his arm but didn't put away his gun. "You've got some nerve," he snarled, walking toward me.

"But let me humor you," he continued, his voice dripping venom. "I was surveilling the place when I saw a shadow moving around in here. So, I thought I'd check it out."

He stopped at the kitchen island, the large counter the only thing separating the two of us. "What about you? Mind telling me what the hell you're doing here? You suddenly blind or something? Didn't see the crime scene tape? This place is blocked off!"

"Jake, it's not what it looks like," I found myself saying. A Hail Mary of sorts.

"Really? What is it then?"

I'm a detective! I can help you! I wanted to scream, tell him everything, make him understand.

I know things you don't. You need me.

"I...I can't explain it," I stuttered, the frustration bubbling in my voice. "But I can help you. I can help you with this case."

"Maybe that overconfident bull crap works in whatever city you came from, but we follow the law around here. That obviously doesn't mean anything to you, but it does to me."

"You don't understand! Let me help you." I looked into his

hardened eyes. I was not one to plead, but I needed Jake to listen to me.

"I know what I'm doing, okay? You just have to trust me," I tried again, softening my voice. My hands were still up as a placating gesture.

Jake cocked his head, studying me. His brows were furrowed, the force of his anger slowly bubbled to the surface. I felt my skin prickle under his gaze.

"Why the hell are you so interested in this case?" he snapped. "And is that why you agreed to go out with me? To ask questions?"

There was no hurt in his voice. He sounded fed up, disgusted with me. And at this moment, I hated myself, too, for agreeing to go out with him.

"What are you up to, Sharon?"

"I'm not the enemy here, Jake."

"How do I know that for sure? You come here out of the blue and start causin' trouble. Why should I believe you?"

"Look, Jake..." I lowered my hands and made a move toward him. To do what, I wasn't sure.

It was the wrong thing to do, though, because Jake lifted his arms and aimed the gun at me again.

"Put your hands up, Sharon! Don't come any closer!"

"Jake, this is not—"

"Enough, Sharon! Hands on your head! You're under arrest for trespassing and possible obstruction of justice," he said, his booming voice echoing around the small, empty cottage.

"You're making a mistake!" I yelled at him, but his gun was still pointed at me. Staring. Menacing.

I could tell from his face he didn't believe anything I said. I knew I had no choice but to put my hands on my head. He whipped out a pair of handcuffs, the silver metal glimmering in the dark.

"Jake, this is not what it looks like!" I tried once more, even though it was useless. Jake grabbed one wrist, then the other, and pulled them behind my back hard.

"I'm telling you right now, I...I...." I felt my heart thundering in my chest. I couldn't blow my cover! But I couldn't go to jail. Either way, I was screwed.

"You're making a mistake! Jake, listen to me!" I pleaded with him as the cold metal of the handcuffs slid against my skin.

"Enough, Sharon!"

I didn't say anything else. Jake didn't either. The next sound I heard was the cuffs closing around my wrists with a sickening click.

MYSTERY ON THE HALF SHELL

A Piper Sandstone Savory Mystery Series, Part 3

By: Karen McSpade

Edited by Darci Heikkinen

Cover Design by Rizwan Noor

15

TAKEN BY SURPRISE

"You're free to go," Jake spat out as if it pained him to say the words. His mouth thinned into a straight line, and his voice turned cold and lifeless. Any trace of his cute, boyish grin was gone.

"Really?"

What a stupid thing to say, but my mouth and brain seemed unable to form any other words as the sheriff twisted a key into the lock of the jailhouse door.

His irritated glare was all the answer I needed. His eyes flashed and darkened with anger like I insulted him. Once warm and calm, his steel-blue eyes were now as menacing as a raging, storm-ridden ocean.

"I mean, yes. Right," I stammered before I completely drowned from the look in his eyes. I got up from the wooden bench in the middle of the jail cell and walked towards him.

He was still in his shirt and sport coat from our "date," but now he wore his badge on a chain around his neck. The metal glinted under the flickering yellow lights.

"Jake...I just—"

"Get your stuff and go," he said, voice dripping venom, not bothering to look at me. He slammed the steel door shut and locked it.

With one final glare, he turned on his heel and walked away. His boots clomped on the tiles until he disappeared.

"Right. Thanks, then," I mumbled into the empty room. Then, not knowing what else to do, I walked around aimlessly, trying to navigate the cold grey hallways of the police station.

How was I even out? Surely, Jake would've made hell rain down on me. His face had contorted into such anger when he saw me snooping in Susan's cottage. I'd never seen him look like that before. Hell, I'd never seen *anyone* look like that before. Granted, breaking and entering wasn't the brightest of ideas, but I just wanted to help. If they knew who I really was, none of this would have happened.

And then there was my chief. And Chicago. Had they heard of this unfortunate incident? Even though it was a small town, the police station still had records, didn't they? And a nationwide system that could be accessed anywhere. Chief Hobbs—uncle or not—would have a conniption. I just hoped he was too busy to keep tabs on me. If he did know, I prayed to God he wouldn't mention this to my dad.

"Don't do anything stupid," the chief told me then, on that bright sunny afternoon in the mall parking lot. Felt just like yesterday. But somehow, also like a decade ago. Like a whole other person ago.

Now here I was, doing the exact thing Chief told me not to do.

"There she is," Doris said in a sing-song voice. Relief rushed through me so strongly that I thought my knees would give out.

It had been a long night, and my head started to feel fuzzy. Did I manage to call the Delta Queens somehow before I was thrown in jail?

"What are you guys doing here?" I asked, trying to act cool. But I hugged each of them tight and hung on like a koala.

"We bailed you out, silly!" cried Patty Sue.

"You were lucky, young lady," Rosemary chimed in. "You just rode the gravy train with biscuit wheels!"

"Just a charge of misdemeanor and a small fine," explained Margie. "Don't worry about it, dear. Let's get you home, get some hot tea in you," she said, patting my arm.

I still wore the off-shoulder blouse from my "date" with Jake. My skin prickled with the cool morning air, and I shivered without realizing it. Margie took off her coat and draped it over my shoulders.

"Been a long night, hm?" Doris asked as we walked to the car. She smiled at me kindly, putting her arms around me to steady me. The exhaustion of the night seeped into my bones, and I wanted to melt into her.

"Yeah. You could definitely say that."

It was sunrise when we finally pulled into Margie's driveway. Once inside, they started fussing over me like I was some sort of toddler. In some ways, that's what I was, a naughty young detective...who had been put in time-out.

"Thank you. All of you. For bailing me out and everything," I said between sips of hot tea. "And for letting me stay. I don't think I want to be alone right now."

"Of course, dear. Think nothing of it. You've been through the wringer," Margie commiserated.

"Yes, it's been...quite interesting." Funny how I thought last night would be a nice, friendly date with Jake. Dinner and a little walk through the park, maybe. Life could really throw you unexpected curve balls sometimes.

"Now, if you don't mind, Sharon sweetheart. Let's get to the nitty-gritty. You were in Susan's cottage, right?" Doris pressed.

"We heard her body was found in the Tombigbee River. It was all everyone in town talked about last night," Rosemary said, eager to hear what I knew.

I heaved a sigh without thinking. Not because I didn't want to answer, but because reliving it again gave me a headache. I did enough of that in the four hours I was locked away, walking back and forth in that 4-by-6-foot cell that smelled like rotten cheese. I rubbed at my pounding temples.

"Yes, Jake got the call when we were having dinner. I rode with him to the river, and...uh, I saw the body. It's definitely her. The dress she was wearing that day, the bracelets. All of it."

"Oh, the poor thing," they tsk-ed, almost in unison.

"Then, I was on my way home, and I passed by the Channing estate. And I saw her cottage," I said, shaking my head. How did I explain without sounding like a complete psycho? "I just...*had* to look. I had to see if I could find any clues to help me...us figure out what happened to Susan."

To my surprise, the four of them nodded their heads solemnly, like they understood completely.

"I'm really sorry if I let you all down," I muttered glumly.

"Nonsense, dearie. You had good reason. You're an

honorary member of the Dentures and Diamonds Crime Squad, after all," said Doris, rubbing my back.

"Susan's cottage looked...normal, or at least as normal as things could be. No signs of struggle or anything. But there were a couple of weird things."

I told them about the note I found, likely scrawled in a panic. And then there was that packed suitcase tucked away neatly beside her bed, ready for...what? A flight to somewhere far away? A quick disappearance? Surely, it wasn't for some weekend getaway jaunt.

"The note said, 'don't go golfing?'" asked Patty Sue, her forehead crinkling at that piece of information.

"Who was that note for? Golfing? How strange," muttered Rosemary. "It's not like it's the most dangerous sport in the world."

I deflated down into the couch like a pierced balloon. None of us had any answers to that.

"Goodness me," sighed Doris, the weight of Susan's death hitting her like a ton of bricks. "And now she's just...gone."

Someone made sure of that. But who?

"Me, oh my. This isn't about a missing dog anymore. It's a full-blown homicide," Margie said as the somber realization of the situation sank in.

Right. Victory. Who was still missing without a trace. If he was with Susan, why wasn't his body found yet? They scoured the river last night, hoping to find him. Was he dead too? I hoped deep down he wasn't. I hoped that poor dog had some fight left in him.

"Well, ladies. Looks like the Dentures and Diamonds Crime Squad is officially back in business. Unfortunate circumstances, of course, but..." Doris said, trailing off.

"We have to narrow down the suspects," I said after a

while. It was what Piper Sandstone would do. I needed to tap into my inner badass detective-ness. "We need a good motive and—"

The radio on the table started sputtering and cracking all of a sudden, making us all jump. A deep, gravelly voice hissed through the large radio transmitter.

...found Susan in the river... the voice started, clearly agitated. There were short bursts of rapid breathing like the person was pacing back and forth.

I sat up and focused on the voice.

...this...not in our plans... It was a male voice, clear as day. We all knew who it belonged to—Adam Kane. My ears perked up. We all looked at each other in shock. Again, with that plan. What are you two scheming? I thought to myself.

...okay, we can...please calm down... came Valorie's smooth voice trying to soothe him.

...I told you to stop saying that... Adam snapped at her, the irritation leaking from his voice and reaching all the way through the radio waves.

Was the plan not to have Susan's body resurface in the Tombigbee River? The ropes, the weights tied to her ankles. Was that the plan?

...won't come back to us... Valorie said, cool and collected. I pictured her reaching for a glass of red wine.

...how do you know that for sure... Adam continued, his voice coming quicker and more erratic. I imagined him flailing his arms around in a panic. He always acted so unflappably, so this was an interesting turn of events.

The radio crackled a bit more, the static sputtering and hissing until we couldn't make out anything else. The last thing we heard was footsteps trailing off as they apparently walked away from the kitchen. Lingering behind, an unsettling silence.

"Those scheming snakes," Rosemary blurted out, her fist banging on the coffee table. "I bet they had something to do with this!"

"Should we tell Jake?" Margie asked.

It was a reasonable enough question, but it still made me jump up from my seat on the couch with a loud "No!"

"I mean, I know we should. It's the right thing to do," I sighed in defeat. "But this will just give him more ammunition against me. If I bring this to Jake out of nowhere, he'll drag me right back to jail. Or maybe to a psych ward."

The ladies all looked at each other and nodded slowly in agreement.

"Plus, the way I planted that bug. Won't exactly bode well for me in a court of law." Honestly. I didn't need another black mark in my already tainted record.

"I'm afraid she's right," Doris added. "Besides, we don't have any concrete information. Just speculations from the bits we've heard on that radio."

"Yes, that definitely makes sense. But...we have to do something about those two, don't we? Find out what they're up to once and for all?" Patty Sue asked, shaking her peacock feather pen at us for emphasis.

"Well," I started, the wheels turning in my head. "We don't really need Jake and the police for that."

16

OPERATION STINGRAY

I'd been through a few stakeouts in my career, and I had to say, this might have been the most boring one. Today was officially day two of Operation Stingray. The mission? Trail Adam Kane and Valorie Channing and find out what they were up to once and for all. The plan was for me to keep a lookout here at the Channing estate, while the Delta Queens would keep their eyes and ears peeled over at the café.

Doris's old Jeep Cherokee was now littered with half-empty Red Bull cans and scrunched-up Doritos bags. On the back seat were more grocery bags filled with junk food. I even had a cooler for my refreshments. After all, I didn't know how long I would be sitting here before they finally came along.

Thankfully, I had the weekend off from the café so I could stay here as long as I wanted. Yesterday, I spent a good sixteen hours on the stakeout, only to go back to Margie's house with nothing to report. Except maybe the number of squirrels I'd counted all over the Channing property. Twenty-nine was the final count. It was sad that I knew that.

"So, this will be a weekend well-spent. Not!" I muttered

under my breath. My back began to ache from all this sitting around. I'd been here since before sunrise and, four hours in, still not a glimpse of either Adam Kane or Valorie Channing. I braced myself for another dreadfully dull day.

"Don't look at me like that," I told Mister, who glared at me from his perch on the front passenger seat. His eyes were little black pools of disdain. Even he was bored out of his mind. If he could cross his paws over his chest, I think he would.

"What? You wanted to come with me."

He tilted his head and furrowed his brows like he understood me and wanted to know what in the world I was talking about. Because no, he did not want to come with me at all.

"Well, I couldn't leave you all alone in the house for so long," I said with a defensive shrug. I didn't mind the company. Having him around beat sitting here by myself.

I was parked a few blocks away from the Channing estate, beneath the cool shade of a large poplar tree. I wasn't far from the spot where I parked when I broke into Susan's cottage that night. It was the perfect location, partially hidden by the tree and hard for oncoming cars to discern before the road curved away from the property. It also offered an ideal sightline to the Channing's gated entrance.

"Surely, they'll be meeting up soon. Right?" I asked Mister. He looked at me intently, tongue hanging out of his mouth like he was trying to figure it out too. "I mean, they'd have to. They were pretty freaked out about the police finding Susan's body."

When they met again, I knew they would be cautious. I'd been listening to the bug for days like an obsessive maniac, waiting for clues, waiting for a slip-up regarding their secret rendezvous. Instead, all I heard were clatters from utensils and the faucet getting turned on and off.

I was sure they would meet here since they'd done it before. With Winston working late most evenings, who was to stop them? I remembered Adam Kane casually rolling into the estate when Valorie kicked me out when I visited her. I also recalled seeing Adam and Valorie in a car together by the side of the road, talking intently. They had to meet again soon; I was sure of it.

"Maybe they have a secret code or something. I mean, whatever they're hiding, they're most likely hiding from the house staff too. They can't just blurt it out loud. What do you think?" I asked Mister.

He stared at me for a second and then started to snuggle into the leather seat to take a nap.

"I'm sorry about this, buddy. We'll get you a nice treat afterward, hm?" I rubbed at the fur on his head, and he gave my hand a little slobbery lick.

Suddenly, his brown floppy ears perked up, and he sat up at attention. His little black nose wiggled as he looked fervently out the window, tail pointing up as if on high alert.

"What is it?"

Then a black sedan pulled up toward the gate and into the driveway. A Chevrolet Malibu I recognized from before. Adam Kane.

Bingo.

I adjusted the driver's seat and shrank down as low as I could go.

"Hide, Mister. Hide!" Mister seemed to get the memo because he sank back down in his seat to avoid being seen through the window.

After a few minutes, I caught sight of the sedan leaving the property. I noted that Valorie was now in the car too.

"Got 'em. Let's hit it, Mister."

As much as I wanted to screech off in hot pursuit *Fast and Furious* style, I knew I had to keep the lowest of low profiles. I maneuvered carefully away from my parking spot and slowly trailed after them, making sure I kept my distance.

We drove past more gargantuan mansions—all tan stucco walls and tall glass windows nestled within manicured landscapes and wrought iron gates. We kept going until the wide stretches of suburban roads narrowed into Savory's charming main street.

I didn't think I'd ever get tired of these quaint streets lined with shops and restaurants. The paved road flanked by old red brick buildings and hand-lettered signs. It was cozy with just the right amount of vintage flair. The streets bustled with people going about their daily business. Families making the most of the sunny day, teenagers hanging around, children shrieking as they played on the sidewalks.

I waited for Adam and Valorie to stop and park somewhere, hoping they wouldn't be straying too far from the town center.

But of course, that would be too easy, wouldn't it?

They kept going, with me trailing not far behind. Before I knew it, we left Savory behind and entered into green swathes of farmland and long stretches of highway. The road was emptier now, and it was harder for me to hide. If they noticed me trailing them, they didn't really seem to do much about it.

"What are you two doing?" I muttered to myself. Mister was on high alert, too, staring out the windshield, tail thumping against the leather seat.

As we drove further away from Savory and onto the interstate, past more gas stations and outlet stores, dread started to sink down my chest. *Are you running away? Why? What did you do?*

My gaze fell to the side view mirror, and a shiver ran down my spine.

"Oh, crap."

Mister turned to me and cocked his head.

"Mister, I think we got a bogie on our tail." My voice turned shaky in an instant, and my palms became slick with sweat.

It was a blink-or-you'd-miss-it moment. But when I caught a glimpse of the shiny black Chevy Silverado behind us, I knew I was in trouble.

Because that truck belonged to Jake.

I would recognize that truck anywhere. It had this huge grill-guard on the front bumper and bright halo headlights. When I clambered on top of it that night at the Tombigbee River, I remembered thinking it looked like a tank.

Did he know who I was following? Had he been waiting by the Channing estate too? He might have been following me since yesterday!

"Dammit!" I wanted to kick myself for not being more careful.

More than anything, I wanted to press on the gas pedal. I wanted to get to Adam and Valorie first and shake them both up until they confessed to whatever they'd done. Or whatever they planned to do. So we could stop with all this craziness, and I could drag them back to the precinct and make Jake understand why I did everything I did.

But I knew I couldn't do it.

I had to play my cards right. Did I let Adam and Valorie

go? Or did I keep going and risk getting caught by Jake? Again.

Adam and Valorie were up to something. If I stayed on their tail, I could stop them. I'd already gone this far. Why stop now?

But then Doris's voice floated back to me, about how all we had were speculations from the bits we had heard on the radio. And I remembered Jake too. How he clenched his jaw and bared his teeth at me, those steel-blue eyes simmering with anger.

If he had been following me since yesterday, then this would be the final nail in the coffin. My coffin. I had to play the long game here. And as much as it pained me to admit it, we didn't have the full story. And it wasn't worth the risk.

"Don't do anything stupid," the chief's warning rang through my head. I rolled my eyes and huffed out a defeated sigh.

A few miles ahead, there was a fork in the road, one that would circle back to the safety of Savory. It was the sign that I needed.

"I'm sorry, Mister. But we have to do this," I said as I turned the steering wheel and left the highway. Adam and Valorie's sedan continued forward until they disappeared completely from view.

Like I predicted, Jake's truck turned, too, following a little further behind me now.

"Well, he can keep trailing us all he wants. But we're going home and stuffing our faces with burgers." At the mention of burgers, Mister's face perked up. "Guess we'll just have to bore him so much that he'll leave us alone, huh?" I told Mister with a pat on his head.

When we finally pulled up to my driveway, the sun had

already set, replaced by a pink and purple haze. I looked around, trying to catch a glimpse of Jake. I couldn't see him, but somehow, I knew he was there, lurking just out of sight. He might have nearly caught me this time, but I was determined to keep at it.

Well. I hate to admit this, but Operation Stingray was a bust.

17

SURPRISE NEWS

I was about to head out the door for a run with Mister
when my phone rang. I barely got the word hello out of
my mouth when a female scream pierced through the
receiver. I recognized Rosemary's panicked voice.

"Rosemary, what's wrong?"

"Sharon!" She let out another blood-curdling scream, and
I could hear a loud clamoring in the background.

"Rosemary, what is it?"

"Sharon, I need you to come to Margie's house right away!
She's got an alligator in her kitchen!"

A what? Did I hear that right?

"What? Are you sure?" She let out another panicked
scream.

"As sure as I'm a 34DD! I'm looking right at it!"

I didn't know what her bra size had to do with this, but I
hoped she was mistaken. "I mean, is there any chance that it's
someone's pet iguana? Those things can get really big."

"This is a full-size alligator, Sharon! And it's rummaging

through Margie's pantry! What should I do? What should I DO?"

"Call animal control now and hang tight, Rosemary. I'll be right over."

I hopped in my car and sped over to Margie's house, my mind reeling with questions—mainly how in the world did an alligator get into Margie's kitchen? And what in the heck could we do about it?

I pulled into the driveway so fast that I almost ran into Margie's garage door before I could stop the car. I sprinted to the front door and braced myself for what I might witness when I opened it.

"Rosemary?" I called out as I entered the house. She was standing on the couch leaning through the large cutaway into the kitchen.

"Oh, thank God you're here, Sharon," she said, pointing through the cutaway. I joined her on the couch and looked through the opening into the kitchen. To my surprise, there was a six-foot alligator pulling a box of Bisquick from Margie's pantry.

"Oh, my God! That's definitely no iguana."

"Well, I told you that."

"Did you call animal control?"

"Yes, and the guy laughed at me like I was some crazy old lady. Then he slammed the phone down. I guess he thought it was a prank."

"But it's not. And look, that thing is making such a mess in Margie's kitchen!"

There were pots and pans strewn across the floor, and we watched in horror as the alligator left large biscuit footprints all over the white tiles. I looked to the left and saw the door to

Margie's patio wide open. "So that's how he got in. Have you called Margie?"

"No, honey, I'm not thinking too clearly. Let's try her now. I've got her on speed dial."

She turned her cell phone on speaker, and we listened as it rang.

"Hello," came Margie's sweet voice on the other end of the receiver.

"Hey, Margie, this is Rosemary and Sharon. Listen, I stopped by your house to drop off the homemade banana pudding I made you. And I hate to tell you this, sugarplum, but you have an alligator in your kitchen. Now, don't panic..."

"Tsk-tsk, that silly Beowulf," Margie laughed. "Did I leave my darn patio door open again?"

"Beowulf? Wait a minute, you know this thing?" I inquired.

"Oh, yes, honey, Beowulf is my neighbor Lucky's pet alligator. He's normally no bother, but I don't let him come into the house. I have a cat, ya know, and they wouldn't get along well at all."

Rosemary and I looked at each other as if we'd just seen a dead person walk by. We were too shocked to know what to say.

After an awkward silence, Margie continued, "I won't be home for another hour or so, but Beowulf loves hot dogs. So if you can get a few out of the refrigerator, you can make a trail right outside the patio door, and he'll be on his way. Make sure the cat doesn't get out, though!"

"Yeah, okay. Sure...we'll try that. Bye now, Margie." Rosemary said in a daze as she hung up the phone.

We stared at each other in complete shock for what

seemed like an eternity. In the background, I could hear Beowulf having a field day in the kitchen.

"Well?" I finally asked.

"Honey, if you think I'm about to try and lure an alligator out that door with a hot dog, you've lost your mind," Rosemary declared.

"Yeah, my thoughts exactly...so, we should...ummm?"

"So, we should run next door and see if we can get Lucky," Rosemary said with a wink.

"Touché, touché! I like the way you think."

Then we burst into laughter as we hopped down from the couch and sprinted over to the neighbor's house.

For a Saturday afternoon at the Crabby Clam Café, it was pretty quiet. The rich, bittersweet aroma of brewing coffee felt like a warm cocoon, engulfing me and making me feel sleepy. The lazy calmness was a welcome distraction from the craziness of the past few days.

Everything seemed to be back to normal, or at least as normal as things could be. Susan's death was still the only thing the whole town could talk about, and everyone seemed to have their own theory of what exactly happened.

As for Jake...well, I hadn't seen him since that close call last weekend. He usually came around for the lunch special on Saturdays, but that obviously wasn't happening now. I didn't know if I felt relieved or disappointed.

I looked around, just a few families having a late brunch. And no screaming kids or toddlers throwing a tantrum. So that was a win for me.

Carla was manning the cash register, so I went around the

tables, asking customers if they needed anything. When I went to work cleaning the trays, I noticed two men by the corner table a few feet away, huddled closely. I recognized them immediately. Winston Channing and Mike Pellegrino.

They were in casual clothes and helping themselves to plates of fried pork chops and mashed potatoes. At first, you'd think they were just two friends having lunch. But they were talking with a serious kind of intensity that made me feel like I was in a company board meeting of some sort.

"I already have contacts set up in Tokyo," I heard Winston say as he chomped on a piece of pork. "And Fukuoka too," he grinned proudly. "Did you know it's called the Silicon Valley in the East? It's a haven for early-stage financial technology startups. "

I pretended to busy myself with the trays while keeping my eyes and ears trained slyly on them. Finally, I saw Mike slowly nod his head in interest.

"What does Richard have to say about it?"

"Nothing yet," answered Winston with a shrewd smile.

"No?"

"Well, I like to get my ducks all lined up in a row first."

Mike took a bite of his mashed potatoes and then rubbed at his stubble, thinking. "I expect he'll have something to say about the deal."

"Once we have everything set, there's nothing more to be done. What I do with my shares is my business," Winston said with a casual shrug.

Then his face turned even more serious, fierce, and determined. "We're looking at the future here, Mike. Online paying platforms and proprietary technology. Richard and I are the same age, sure, but he doesn't share my vision. He doesn't want to move forward. Doesn't want to take risks. Doesn't want to invest in other ventures. I—"

I was so busy eavesdropping that I didn't notice the unsteady stack of trays sliding off the table and landing on the floor with a loud clatter. Every head in the café whipped over to my direction.

"Everything okay?" Mike asked, his bushy eyebrows raised to his hairline.

"Yes, yes. Sorry about that. Just...a case of the clumsy," I chuckled meekly. I picked up the trays, and the pair went right back to their conversation. Luckily, they didn't think much of it. Didn't suspect the clumsy waitress was really an undercover detective eavesdropping on them.

"I have to say, Winston. I'm impressed," I heard Mike say as I crouched down on the cold tiles to pick up the trays. "I believe we share the same vision."

"So, will you accept?"

I wasn't looking at them, but I could tell Mike had this wolfish sort of grin—like he wanted to keep Winston on his toes.

"Give me a few days to think about it."

18

PARTY LIKE A PELLEGRINO

The Pellegrino home wasn't as grand as the Channing mansion, but it still wasn't anything to scoff at. If the Channings had a stately manor, the Pellegrinos owned a more modern and stylish home, all clean lines and geometric shapes. The tiles were a sleek marble, and the walls a spotless white. Yet, despite the clean, minimalist setting, it was anything but sterile.

A small stage was set up in the middle of the living room, where a jazz quartet played their mellow tunes. Guests spilled out from the living room all the way to the manicured garden. Waiters in elegant white tuxes scuttled around, bearing trays filled with champagne flutes and fancy hors d'oeuvres.

Caviar and crème fraîche tartlets? Figs with bacon and chile? It was hardly the usual fanfare for a birthday party. For me, anyway.

"Wow, the Pellegrinos went all out, didn't they?" I said to Patty Sue. She didn't seem fazed by the fanciness of it all.

"Well, it's not every day Mike Pellegrino turns sixty. And

they're relatively new in town, compared to the generations of families living here. They've always been pretty private, too, so I guess they're trying to create a splash."

Splash was right. Nearly all of Savory was here. I spotted Winston amongst a cluster of men in business suits. Valorie looked bored as she sipped champagne with a group of well-dressed women, all in varying versions of the same Chanel gown. Richard Price was by the bar speaking to another gentleman, his face serious and solemn as always. I even saw young Carl munching on hors d'oeuvres like winning his next soccer game depended on it. Yes, it did seem a rather odd and lavish party for a couple who preferred to keep to themselves.

Almost everyone I'd met since I moved to Savory was here. Well, except for Jake. Or maybe he was lurking in the shadows. It was hard to tell.

"Patty Sue! Glad you could make it. It's been so long!" said an unknown woman, pulling Patty Sue into a tight hug. Then came another and another, until she was devoured by a small crowd asking how she was and why she hadn't returned their calls and what had she been up to these days.

"Wow, Patty Sue knows everyone, doesn't she?" I asked Margie as we navigated through the packed crowd for a drink.

"Oh yes. She was quite the social butterfly back in her day. She's stepped back from it, though. All those glitzy parties and hobnobbing with the rich and famous, I suppose it gets tiresome after a while."

"I can only imagine," I replied. It definitely made sense. Ten minutes of faking smiles and making small talk had already left me drained and wanting a nap.

"She's got a lot of tricks up her sleeve, that one. You'd be surprised."

I looked back at her. She was talking in the middle of the crowd, arms waving around intently. Everyone was enthralled. In her bright pink pantsuit and Hermes scarf, Patty Sue looked every bit the cool, eccentric aunt.

I got myself a drink at the bar, content to just stand there and people watch. The buzzing of lively chatter was intense. Strangers bustled around, flitting from the packed living room to the garden, champagne flutes in hand. The music had turned to more sultry jazz.

From the corner of my eye, I saw Mike and Tina Pellegrino step into the living room from the open foyer, immediately swarmed by crowds of well-wishers. Mike was in a tux with Tina by his side, wearing an elegant dark green sheath dress. They looked like one of those old-school Hollywood couples.

Mike made his way to the small stage where the band played and took hold of the microphone. Then, the music stopped, and everyone gathered around the living room.

"Thank you all so much for taking the time to come and celebrate with us," he started. "There's really so much to be grateful for. My beautiful wife Tina, of course. This amazing town that has welcomed us with open arms. We've had so many amazing opportunities here in Savory," he said as applause burst around the room.

"And of course, my new partnership with Winston Channing and Richard Price. I'm really excited about this. This is an incredible venture to be involved with, and I am truly honored," he said, raising his champagne glass for a toast. "To Savory and beyond!"

"Hear, hear!" the crowd chanted.

"New partnership? What does that mean?" Doris whispered, sidling beside me.

Partnership? Venture? Could this be what they were talking about in the café a week ago?

"Oh! I heard them talking about this last week. Something about Winston selling half of his stakes of the business to Mike. And something about Tokyo. I think he'll be starting a business overseas?"

As Mike stepped down from the stage, Winston gave him a little hug, those macho ones where they clap each other's backs. "Well, looks like Mike's all in," Doris murmured.

"What is it?" Rosemary hissed into my ear as the rest of the Delta Queens found their way to us. "What are you talking about? What's happened?"

"Well, it looks like we have a new big fish in town."

19

MISSION IMPOSSIBLE

"Did you hear? Did you hear?" Doris said, bursting into my front door, the rest of the Delta Queens hot on her trail.

"Susan's autopsy report has been released!" Rosemary burst out excitedly before I could respond.

Doris rolled her eyes fondly and gave a little shrug. "Granted, it's not the best thing to be excited about, but it's definitely something."

It had been almost two weeks since the discovery of Susan's body, and the trail was turning cold. The leads had been thin if there were any at all. The investigators had combed through the area surrounding the Tombigbee River, through the edges of the nearby swampy black water, looking for traces of DNA: fingerprints, hair, blood—anything, hoping to find clues on the killer. So far, nothing.

Now, I wasn't an expert in forensic science, but I would have to admit, finding anything would be near impossible. The area was vast, with thick foliage that would perfectly hide any shred of evidence. The killer knew what they were doing.

All of us were getting antsy, eager for more information. This report could shine new light on the case and maybe present some further clues about what happened to Susan.

"Well, we have to get our hands on that report," I concluded. I knew postmortem results were public records, but I wasn't sure since the investigation was still ongoing.

"We could sneak into the hospital. Disguise ourselves in scrub suits!" Margie said excitedly.

"Oh, oh! I'll pretend to be a patient! You can put me in one of those wheelchairs. I can definitely pull off those ghastly hospital gowns," Rosemary added with that signature smirk of hers.

"We could get blueprints of the hospital floor plans! Get those earpiece things and go in like that handsome fella from *Mission Impossible*," Margie said, her eyes gleaming at the thought of being a secret agent.

"You've been watching too many movies," Doris said, wrinkling her nose.

"Or..." Patty Sue started. "I could use my connections from the hospital to get us this," she said, producing a thick sheaf of papers enclosed in a brown folder. The hospital seal was stamped on the cover.

"What the...?" I stuttered.

"How? What?" Margie said, a little disappointed she wouldn't be sneaking around the hospital.

"Connections, my dear. Quid pro quo and all that."

"You didn't tell us you had that!" Doris said almost indignantly.

"I was waiting for the right moment," Patty Sue answered. "For the dramatic effect and everything."

As excited as we were to see the report, there was nothing in it that we didn't know already. Cause of death was drowning. The rope tied around her waist, the weights that held her down, how she was left to sink down into the riverbed. It was painfully evident that someone didn't want her to be found.

"She must have been dragged to that lake kicking and screaming," Doris said sadly after a few beats of silence. She couldn't stomach reading the entire report, turning her head away when the pictures of her body appeared on the pages.

As if on autopilot, my brain went back to those pictures of the murdered drug dealer I saw when I was still Piper Sandstone. I would never forget those pictures. I didn't think I'd ever forget these either.

"She didn't go down without a fight, that Susan. It said here there were signs of struggle," Margie said, skimming the report. "Mm-hmm...oh...okay. Well, it does appear she fought like hell."

Of course, she fought like hell. I didn't know her, but I could tell Susan was strong. She wasn't weak, by any means. It was this cold-blooded killer who was weak. And a coward. Who was also, unfortunately, still on the loose.

Before I could give it any more thought, I found myself blurting out, "I'm going back to the river. To look for more clues. We need more evidence. There must be something the police have overlooked."

It wasn't an impulsive decision, which I admitted I was prone to every now and again. But going there, doing this, looking for more clues—it felt right. Because everything else about this case just felt so, so...wrong.

"Makes you feel uneasy, huh?" Doris said, still with that sad voice of hers, like she could read my thoughts.

I nodded slowly. I looked out the window and watched Mister dig more holes in my already messy backyard.

"We can't bring her back, but justice has to be served. Finding out who did this to her, it's the least we can do."

Susan was close to my age. And she lived a happy life here in Savory, with friends and family who loved her. For all that to be just ripped away in the blink of an eye. To know she met such a tragic end in that murky river. It made me feel queasy, made my stomach flip with a quiet, simmering rage. And apparently, I wasn't the only one.

Doris stood up quickly and grabbed her jacket and the keys of her Jeep. "Well, let's go then."

"Wait, what?" I stammered. Not quite the reaction I was expecting.

"Well, my dear. We're going with you!" Patty Sue said, patting my cheek and already heading out the door. "We'll be like those agents in *Mission Improbable* after all."

"It's Mission Impossible, dear," Doris laughed.

"Five pairs of eyes are better than one, sweetheart," Margie smiled at me softly. "Let's do this."

Everyone was quiet in the car. Doris insisted that she would do the driving, which I was grateful for since that meant I could be on the lookout. I kept my eyes locked on the side view mirror. I tried not to blink too much. Then I'd subtly turn my head to look at the rearview mirror. And then back to the side view one. I also poked my head out the window for good measure. If someone was on our tail, I'd catch them.

"No one's following us, Sharon. It's okay," said Doris softly.

"Yes, right." I let out a breath I didn't know I was holding and relaxed my tensed-up shoulders.

"You just never know. Gotta stay on your toes," I chuckled weakly. Doris just hummed in response, but I knew she knew what was on my mind. Jake wasn't just suspicious anymore. He was angry too. And if he caught on to what we were really doing, even just a whiff, then the jig would be up.

And this wasn't just about me attempting to solve town mysteries with the Dentures and Diamonds Crime Squad. I still had a secret no one in this town knew about. I was still Piper Sandstone, undercover cop for the Chicago police force, thrown into Savory against my will. I was still in hiding. My secret could never get out. Not if I wanted to have a career as a detective when I got out of here.

But Jake was like a dog with a bone. He wasn't letting go. I discreetly glanced out the side view mirror again and breathed into the pitch-black darkness.

The night breeze was cool against my cheek, a far cry from the suffocating humidity the last time I was here. The trees rustled softly with the wind. The moon was a perfect crescent, the silver light reflecting against the murky water of the Tombigbee River. I looked up at the stars dotting the sky. It would have been the perfect night for a walk...if this were another time.

Margie let out a full-bodied shiver. "Ugh. Big bodies of water make me feel all iffy and weird."

I thought the river looked pretty. The water was shiny and illuminating, almost inviting. I suddenly remembered the restaurant by the port where Jake and I had dinner. And then, of course, the sight of Susan's body being dragged out of this same river, seaweed tangled around her legs. I let out a shiver too.

"There must be something around here. Maybe tire tracks? Footprints?" Doris said as we walked around the river to the edges of the marshy swamp. "Even the best cold-blooded killer makes mistakes sometimes."

"Only one way to find out," I said, taking out my flashlight. "Let's see how good our mystery killer is."

We walked and walked into the thick clusters of trees until the ground turned wet and muddy. The leafy canopy of the forest stretched up and up above us, blocking away all traces of moonlight. I focused on the chirping of the crickets and the croaking of the frogs to ground myself.

"Looks like footprints are out. Tire tracks too. Any of those would have been washed away by now," Patty Sue said, looking at our muddy footprints trailing behind us. I didn't even know which parts of the area had already been scoured by the police.

"Maybe Susan was able to leave something of hers behind? A shoe, a hair tie? Like little trails of crumbs," said Margie thoughtfully.

"Yes, we can't rule those out," I said. We were so deep into the swampland that finding anything would have been nothing short of a miracle. We couldn't lose hope, though. "If there weren't any tire tracks, they must have walked on foot. Was she already tied up then? Or did she go here willingly?"

"If she did, she must have been with someone she trusts," Doris concluded.

"If it was someone she knew, then that means—"

"Shh! Oh my God! Do you hear that?" Rosemary

suddenly shout-whispered. She stood rooted to her spot, eyes wide and flitting from side to side.

"What? What?"

And then I heard it too. A rustling of leaves, faint at first, but it grew louder and louder every second. Footsteps crunching against the leaves. Whatever it was, it was getting closer, and it was big.

Crap! Crap!

"Oh, Lord! Hide! Hide," Margie whined, diving into a thick bush behind her. It wasn't the best hiding spot, but there was no time to think. Before I knew it, we were all jumping in with her and crouching behind the big leaves.

"Oh my God! It's the Loch Ness monster!" Rosemary whispered, her voice trembling.

"Loch Ness? When did we get on a plane and fly to Scotland, then?" Doris asked in her calm, reassuring voice.

"The Loch Ness monster wouldn't really appreciate our swamp water here, that's for sure," said Patty Sue in a serious tone.

As the sound grew even closer, I *wished* it was the Loch Ness monster. What if it were Jake and the whole squadron of Savory's finest police officers? What if he followed us after all? And it wouldn't be just me who'd get in trouble. The Delta Queens were right here with me!

Oh, Chief Hobbs would have a field day. Like it wasn't enough that I did something so colossally stupid. I had to bring four perfectly innocent senior civilians down with me.

Even worse, what if it were the mystery killer coming to finish us off? What if they'd been sitting here and waiting all along? Preying on whoever was brave—or idiotic—enough to come here?

Dammit, why didn't I bring my gun?

"Well, you mind telling me what in the fresh hell is that?" hissed Rosemary.

All of us held our breaths as the footsteps grew closer and closer. The sound was now soft and light, which was weird. What kind of killer had such delicate steps?

The sounds stopped just a few feet from where we were hiding. I wanted to take a quick peek and see what we were up against, but I opted to just brace myself for whatever it was. I balled up my fists as the footsteps moved toward the bush.

And then, an odd-shaped face peeked around the side of the foliage, looking like a dark gray cloud. If it weren't for the black, beady eyes staring right at us and its black nose, I'd have thought it was just a puff of smoke.

What in the world? Was this some kind of weird fever dream? Did a mosquito bite us? Send us into a malaria-induced haze?

The mysterious head tilted to the side. Inched toward us slowly, footsteps pattering against the earth. We waddled backward on instinct, still crouching. The fluff ball had mud all over it, all over its tall, spindly legs and long body, even up on the poof on top of its head.

What the...? Was it...a hyena? A jackal? Were jackals a thing around these parts?

"Oh. My. God," Rosemary whispered slowly from the corner of her mouth, not taking her eyes off it. "It's a...swamp creature."

No one dared move an inch. Instead, we braced ourselves for the worst, waited for a snarl, a growl, the sharp glint of pointy teeth, a loud, sickening howl.

But it never came.

The creature just kept looking at us, regarding us with

curiosity. Then it tilted its head slowly. Almost shyly. And that's when recognition hit me like a freight train.

"Lost dog" flyers plastered all over Savory when he first disappeared. His picture and the Channings' number written on the paper. That tilt of his head. The exact same one that was in the photo.

"Oh my God! That's Victory!"

20

SHELL SHOCKED

"We have to talk to Winston and Valorie. Now." My voice was weirdly steely. The words came out as soon as the maid pulled the door open.

"Um, what...what is this about?" she asked nervously. It was the same young woman from before, from the day I planted the bug in Valorie Channing's kitchen. Now, she looked shell-shocked, clearly not expecting a small army ringing the doorbell in the middle of the night.

Rosemary stepped out from behind me and pointed to the poodle standing at her hip. Victory gave a happy bark and wagged his tail playfully.

"Well, we just found their long-lost dog. No big deal."

"Oh! Oh my," the maid said with a gasp. "Well, why didn't you start with that? Come on in, then. Come on in," she said, frantically waving us inside.

A good splash of water from the river and Victory looked like a standard poodle again. Somewhat. He was still caked with mud on his back end, but we managed to get it off his face, so white tufts of fur sprouted out. With an old blanket draped over him, it looked like we were smuggling an alien into the Channing mansion.

As we walked through the hallway leading to the main living room, we heard voices deep in conversation. The maid stopped us with a hushed whisper. "I'm afraid they're in the middle of a meeting with Mr. Price right now. Maybe you could wait for—"

"Nonsense," Rosemary huffed, walking past her. "This is their dog we're talking about, dearie."

With a shrug, we all followed her into the entryway of the living room, the maid calling out after us.

"Wait, wait!" she snapped. But it was not like we were ones to listen.

At the far end of the living room, lounging by the over-sized sofa, sat Winston and Valorie. The space was so large that they didn't even notice us coming in. They were too busy anyway, listening to Richard Price.

The imposing figure had his back to us, looking out the window, a lit cigar dangling between his fingers. With the sharp black suit and sleek silver hair, he didn't even have to turn around for me to recognize him. Something about Richard and his Godfather-like silhouette sent a shiver down my spine.

"And I gotta say, Winston," he said in that smooth, rich voice of his. "Once we close in on those deals and set up banks in Riverside, you can finally upgrade this old house of yours and—"

He was cut off by Victory's excited yip. All three heads whipped toward us so fast I was surprised none of them got whiplash.

"What the—" Winston stammered. Valorie's jaw almost

unhinged from her mouth at the sight of the blanketed animal Rosemary led into the room.

At first, Richard didn't seem to register what was going on. His eyes flitted from side to side, brows furrowed, studying this motley crew that appeared before him, wondering why in the world one of us barked like that. When his gaze fell upon Victory, the cigar in his hand dropped to the floor with a teensy thud, the grey ash smattering all over the pristine marble floor.

"Victory?" Valorie managed to squeak out. "Oh my God!"

Valorie and Winston leaped from their seats and rushed to us, cooing over Victory.

"Where did you find him?" Winston asked, lifting the blanket from Victory and reaching down to hug him close to his chest, caked mud and all.

"Down by the river. He was wandering around," I answered. There would probably be a lot of questions regarding our discovery of Victory. We'd have to keep it simple.

"He was so cold and hungry, the poor thing. He probably got caught up in the swamp since he was so muddy when we found him. We wrapped him up in blankets and gave him some food," Doris added.

"Oh, look at you. You sweet, messy boy," Valorie cooed, rubbing at Victory's dirty, matted fur.

Was that...emotion on Valorie Channing's face? She always looked so bored, so jaded, like she wanted to be somewhere else. I had never even seen a smile cross her face—until now. Maybe Victory has thawed her icy heart.

"Why were you..." Richard spoke suddenly, clearing his throat. "Why were you down by the river so late in the evening?"

"Oh, you know," Rosemary chuckled. "The gals and I needed some fresh air, and slogging through the mud is good exercise. Gotta keep the legs looking trim," she said, giggling in what I thought was her attempt at flirting.

Slogging through the mud? I would have laughed at Rosemary's half-baked excuse if not for Winston drawing our attention back to Victory.

"Well, thank you very much for bringing our dear Victory home," Winston said, voice still slightly breaking.

"It's a shame he wasn't found earlier," Valorie drawled. "The Westminster Dog Show is in a couple of days. Unfortunately, he won't be able to make it in time, especially without his handler."

The dog show? Wasn't Victory's health and well-being more important? The poor thing must have been traumatized. The warmth in Valorie's eyes from a few minutes ago was gone now, replaced by her usual detached iciness. Figuring out Valorie's mercurial moods was a headache in itself.

"Well," I said brightly. "At least the other dogs there have a chance now."

"Mmm, I suppose," she hummed. Then, with a final glance at Victory, she turned around and poured herself a generous glass of red wine.

"Well, then. It's quite late. I'll be off," Richard said after an awkward pause filled the room. He gave Winston and Valorie quick hugs. "Valorie, always a pleasure. Winston, we'll talk some more about Riverside at lunch this week."

"Definitely, definitely. Drive safe, Richard," Winston said, clapping him on the back.

"Ladies?" Richard said, turning his attention to us. Rosemary nearly melted into a puddle on the spot. "It's been a pleasure. Thank you for bringing Victory back."

"Of course. Glad we were able to help," I said.

His icy blue eyes seemed to bore into me. When he smiled, his canine teeth shone under the light. "Have a good evening, ladies."

"Goodbye, Mr. Price."

Through the window, I watched him leave the house. Before he even finished climbing down the steps, a sleek, silver BMW purred into the driveway, waiting.

Hmm. That's weird.

The car looked vaguely familiar, like a memory just out of reach. Of course, Savory was a small town, and there weren't a lot of luxury cars just parading around.

Maybe I'd seen it before parked in front of the Crabby Clam Café? Passed by it when I went jogging? No, no. That didn't feel quite right.

The car door was held open by a young man who also looked painfully familiar. Pimply faced with a wispy mustache and an ill-fitting suit. Permanent scowl on his face. I felt myself scrunch up in concentration. I'd seen him before; I was sure of it.

That kid from the pet store! Of course! He nearly ran over me, sent my pet supplies flying into the air. Not even an apology from that punk.

Funny. I'd yet to ask the Delta Queens about him.

21

HIGH ANXIETY

"Sharon! You work here?" said Winston Channing, pleasantly surprised as soon as he saw me approach their table. Valorie sat beside him, an almost sullen expression on her face. So much for Victory thawing her cold heart.

I was surprised to see them since I rarely saw the Channing couple out and about together, and I had never seen them dine at the Crabby Clam Café. Tonight, though, they were joined by Mike Pellegrino.

"Yes, yes I do. How are you today, Mr. Channing?"

"Not bad, not bad at all. Again, we can't thank you enough for finding Victory."

"That was really great work you gals did," said Mr. Pellegrino, his toothy wide grin infectious. "I heard all about it. I'm more of a cat person myself, but Victory is a sweetheart."

"Of course. It was a lucky coincidence. I'm just so glad he's back safe and sound," I said through gritted teeth. Traipsing through swampland looking for clues was anything but luck. But they didn't have to know that. That last part was true, though. Victory was a wonderful dog.

"Well, we should have you over for dinner sometime. You and the whole gang," Winston said, looking at me in earnest. "Wouldn't that be nice, sweetheart?" he said, turning to Valorie.

"Hm? Yes, yes. That would be quite lovely," Valorie said, fidgety and distracted. She wasn't even looking at me, her eyes constantly flicking to the tables on her right. She must have caught me staring because she straightened up and looked intently at the menu in front of her like I would be quizzing her on it afterward.

"So, um, what are the specials for tonight, Sherry?"

"It's Sharon."

"Mmm," she hummed, the uneasiness coming off of her like waves. She cleared her throat. "The Oysters Rockefeller sound good. Are those fresh?

"Of course. Those are brought in fresh right from the Gulf Shores. They are delicious and savory if that's your thing."

"Yes, yes. I'll have those. And your best bottle of Sauvignon Blanc," she said, handing me back the menu brusquely.

If Winston noticed Valorie's fidgeting, he didn't comment on it. "The lamb ribs for me, please. Thanks so much, Sharon."

"I'll have my usual, the seafood gumbo," added Mike. "Pretty busy night, huh?" he said, looking around the packed restaurant. The place was buzzing with loud chatter.

"Oh yes. Friday nights are always the craziest," I smiled politely at him. I looked around the restaurant as well, my eyes searching for the Delta Queens like I always did. It took a few seconds for me to remember that they were out of town visiting a friend and would be back on Monday.

"Right, well. I'll be back in a bit with your dinners," I said, smiling brightly at them as they resumed their conversation, which was honestly just Winston and Mike talking business while Valorie squirmed in her seat.

What is with her? She's acting like having dinner here is a death sentence. Is the Crabby Clam Café not fancy enough for her highbrow tastes?

I glided through the crowd of tables, picking up requests for more napkins or new cutlery. A deep, gravelly voice from the bar counter caught my attention.

"Excuse me. Miss?"

"Yes? Oh! Mr. Price. How can I help you?" Richard Price was sitting atop the corner stool, hidden away from view. He looked particularly dashing today, wearing a three-piece gray suit that complemented his blue eyes. If Rosemary were here, she'd be openly gawking at him.

"Can I get more sparkling water, please?"

"Yes, sure thing. Right away," I managed to say without a stammer. I wasn't quite sure what it was, but the man was so intimidating. Maybe it was the fancy suit. Before I could turn on my heel to get him his water, he spoke again.

"You're the girl from the night before," he said, looking at me intently. "The one who found Victory."

His stare was piercing. I didn't think he remembered me. I mean, why on earth would he even remember me?

"Yep. That's us," I said proudly, forcing out a grin.

"Well," he paused, looking at me strangely before continuing, "Good job," he said finally, with a solemn nod of his head.

"Oh. Thanks! I'll be right back with your water," I said, turning to leave before he could say anything more.

I didn't know he felt so strongly about Victory's disappearance. Maybe he was a big fan.

When I brought over Valorie's steaming plate of oysters, the two men around her barely noticed, still so engrossed in their conversation. Not that Valorie seemed to mind or care. Her elbow was up on the table, chin plopped squarely on her palm, probably feeling as invisible as she looked.

"Here you go. Oysters Rockefeller. Thanks for waiting," I said. Only then did Winston and Mike stop their conversation to ogle at the food.

"Mmm, oysters," hummed Winston appreciatively. He squeezed a little lemon juice over one of the half-shells and then speared at it with the tiny oyster fork to get the freshly baked meat.

"Here you go, sweetheart," he said, bringing the fork to Valorie's lips. "You know oysters are very powerful aphrodisiacs?" he asked with a sly little smile that made him look so much younger.

Valorie curled her lip and begrudgingly opened her mouth to accept the oyster.

"Get a room, you two," Mike guffawed before heartily digging into his gumbo.

"Well, then. Enjoy!" I beamed, turning around to hustle back to the kitchen. I didn't make it five steps when a slight shattering sound stopped me in my tracks. It was from a few tables over to my right.

"Everything okay over there?" I called out to the blonde man sitting alone at the table. His back was to me, so I couldn't see his face, but on the floor beside him were tiny shards of glass glittering in the light.

"Everything's fine," he gritted out. "I...I dropped the glass. Sorry about that."

"That's no problem. We'll get that cleaned up, and oh—"

I stifled a gasp and schooled my expression to be neutral. Because the blonde man was Adam Kane. Of course, I should have recognized that beautiful mop of blonde hair.

"Oh," I said simply. "Mr. Kane."

Adam Kane—in the same place where Valorie Channing was dining. Surely that couldn't be a coincidence? So, I did all that staking out only to have them fall right into my lap? Oh, this is too good.

Dang it, why aren't the Delta Queens here?

"Sharon," he said casually like we were buddies. He was wringing his hands on a napkin, faint traces of blood smearing on the cloth. "Sorry about that. It slipped out of my hand."

Slipped? It looked like it shattered right out of his hand!

"Are you okay?"

"I'm fine, I'm fine," he said, waving me off. "Just a little scratch."

His face and neck were flushed, and I could tell he was trying to rein in his emotions. The pain from the cuts in his hand? Or was it rage that made him break the glass? Whatever it was, I had no clue.

"I'll get someone to clean this up," I said, scampering off before he could reply.

I was on my way to get Carla when another sound caught my attention, this time a panicked shout from the other side of the room.

"Mike?" the voice yelled. It was Valorie.

"Mike! Mike!" A deeper voice this time, equally panic-stricken. Winston.

I ran back to their table, just in time to see Mike's face slumped down in his bowl of gumbo, the stew sloshing to the side and pouring over the edge of the bowl. His hand was clutching at his chest, clawing desperately.

"Oh my God! Help him!" I heard someone yell. Then I realized it was me. It was my distraught voice piercing the air... through the chaos. What was happening?!

KILLER GUMBO

A Piper Sandstone Savory Mystery Series, Part 4

By: Karen McSpade

Edited by Darci Heikkinen

Cover Design by Rizwan Noor

This is a work of fiction. Names, characters, places, and incidents either are products of the author's imagination or are used fictitiously. Any similarity to actual events or locales or persons,
living or dead, is entirely coincidental.

22

HIGH ANXIETY, PART 2

W hat is happening?

Everything blurred into slow motion, going too slow and too fast at the same time, like a weird, hazy dream. I heard the sound of my voice yelling for help, but it seemed like it was coming from miles away.

"Help! Somebody! Call 911!" I heard Winston yelling, too, his chair scraping the floor like nails across a blackboard as he shot up from his seat.

In a panic, I slapped at my apron and then at the pockets on the backside of my jeans. *Dammit! My phone... where the hell is my cell phone?*

"Carla, call 911 and then call Mr. B!" I shouted as I stepped in front of the Channings' table to give them some privacy from the curious crowd.

Then as if he suddenly turned boneless, Mike slumped to the side and fell off his chair, landing on the ground with a sickening thud. His face was pale, turning an alarming shade of blue. His eyes were wide with panic. I looked for signs that he was breathing, but his chest was motionless.

I felt icy hot from the adrenaline, but somehow, I was stuck in place. From where I stood, I could see Winston's arms pumping at his chest, pressing hard and fast. Carla's mouth was moving, trying to blurt out our location to the 911 dispatcher. Valorie's tears streamed down her cheeks. Strangers crowded around, circling us, putting their hands over their mouths in horrified shock. The rich, thick stew of the gumbo made its way along the crevices of the tiles, like a snail through molasses.

"C'mon, Mike. C'mon." I could hear Winston chanting under his breath as he pushed and pushed at Mike's chest.

"25, 26, 27..." he counted, going and going until I couldn't make out what he was saying anymore. Mike's chest rose and fell with every push, no longer breathing on his own.

"C'mon, Mike. C'mon," Winston said again, getting more and more desperate. Sweat was beading from his forehead, arms twitching from the effort. My mouth was moving, too, chanting along with him. I used my arms as a barricade to keep the other diners away. From a distance, I could hear the siren of an ambulance growing closer and closer.

C'mon, Mike. The ambulance is almost here. Just hold on. Hold on for a few more minutes.

His eyes seemed to grow heavier and heavier, his body becoming even slacker than before, melting into the sticky linoleum tiles. He let out a wheezing gasp, and I thought the CPR was working its magic.

Then, like a thick velvet curtain descending upon a stage, his glassy eyes closed.

~

It was an ordinary Friday. Gumbo day. The last day to get through before the weekend. Just like any other Friday before that.

At least, it was supposed to be.

There was nothing different. Just the usual crowd of diners heartily digging into their food, decompressing after a long workweek. There were families tucked into the retro-style booths, chattering loudly. Lovesick couples gazing into each other's eyes at the two-seater tables. Men in suits by the bar counter near the kitchen nursing a drink or two. Richard Price sipping his sparkling water and looking as dashing as always. Carla and all the other servers bustling around with trays of food.

Sure, the Channings weren't really regulars at the Crabby Clam, so maybe that was a little different. But it wasn't like small-town Savory had a bevy of five-star restaurants for them to choose from. And Mike was a well-known gumbo fanatic around these parts anyway, so maybe he insisted on having their dinner-slash-business meeting here.

And there was Adam Kane too. Granted, he was a regular, but why was he acting so weird and huffy? Did he drop the glass or break it with his hand? Was he the reason why Valorie was fidgety during dinner? Did she not want him here? Or was it the opposite? Were they fighting? Why were they acting like strangers? Those two always seemed to be a thorn in my side.

"It was a heart attack, wasn't it?" Carla said. I didn't even notice she was standing next to me.

"That's how one of my uncles died, God bless his soul," she added, and then quickly did a sign of the cross. "Just keeled over like that."

Seemed plausible. People died from heart attacks all the

time. Surely, this had nothing to do with all the weirdness going on in Savory, right? Right?

The thought gnawed at my brain as Carla and I watched the paramedics take away Mike's body on a sheet-draped gurney. Outside the restaurant, the overhead lights of the ambulance kept blinking and flashing, bright red reflecting on the glass windows, creating an eerie glow inside the café. At least the wailing sound of the siren had been turned off.

There wasn't much for us to do except stand there and watch. And wait. The police rushed over along with the paramedics, instructing the shocked crowd not to leave until they had taken their witness statements.

"And he didn't complain about feeling sick? Or in pain?" I heard Jake's voice from where he was talking to the Channings near the kitchen.

And there was that situation with Jake too. I opted to keep out of his crosshairs for the time being since it didn't look good for me that I was there when Mike died. I didn't want another black mark against me. Dear God, please let it be another officer taking my statement.

I slowly made my way to the bar counter and pretended to be busy. I still needed to eavesdrop after all. I couldn't see their faces, but I could hear Winston, sounding smaller than I had ever heard him.

"No, not at all," Winston answered, his voice still slightly hoarse from yelling. "It was just like he had trouble breathing all of a sudden. Before that, he was in pretty good spirits. If anything, he was excited about his gumbo," he chuckled sadly.

Jake paused, possibly taking notes on his pad. "Any medical history of heart problems that you're aware of?"

I pictured Winston and Valorie looking at each other and shaking their heads.

"Not that we know of," said Valorie. "He's very healthy. No alcohol or cigarettes. Clean eating and regular exercise, you know? It's just the kind of person he is...."

A moment of silence dawned on them like a thick fog.

"Was," she corrected herself, her voice soft and shaky. Then her tears came, coming hard and fast with fitful sobs until she was gasping for breath. I could hear Winston rubbing her back, trying to soothe her.

Whatever I thought of Valorie, I knew she was close with Mike. Watching the life drain right out of your friend was indeed a devastating blow.

"It'll be okay. Everything will be okay," I heard Winston murmuring as he clutched Valorie to his chest.

I stared at the steady blinking lights outside, long enough for them to give me a headache. I felt the heavy exhaustion creep up my spine, all the way to my muscles and bones, straight to the marrow. It had been a long day and an even longer night.

I hoped Winston was right.

23

MIDAS TOUCH

"And then he just...fell," I finished, sputtering out the words, not knowing what else to say. In Margie's living room, at the break of dawn, everything seemed to be happening in slow motion—my delayed reaction to the awful event, I assumed.

The Delta Queens raced back home straight away as soon as I told them the news. Now they were sitting on the edge of the couch, mouths agape, leaning toward me, taking in every word of my story.

"But...how could he just...just...?" Doris stuttered.

"I...I...don't know," I answered. I rubbed at my temples like I'd been doing for the past few hours, hoping the answer would just come to me out of the blue. Unfortunately, none of this made any sense.

With Victory being found, it seemed like we finally had a grip on things. Then this happened. Always one thing or another, sending us into a tailspin.

"They think it was a heart attack," I said, almost a whisper.

The room filled with silence again. And when no one else spoke, Rosemary interjected, "But...I don't know. Mike was fit as a fiddle. No family history, either. Winston and Valorie said so. And they've known him for years, even before he and Tina moved here."

Mike did look fit. He didn't have that beer belly that usually accompanied men as they grew older. No vices. Knew how to take care of himself. Of course, you could live an extremely healthy lifestyle and still have a heart attack anyway. Probably the universe being sarcastic.

But still. Something about this didn't sit right.

There was silence again as everyone felt consumed by their thoughts.

"Dare I say...foul play?" asked Patty Sue. Well, it was what everyone had been thinking. Might as well get it out in the open.

"Think it's the same person who killed Susan?" asked Margie.

"Susan and Mike? What's the connection? What do they have in common?" I said. That was what I'd been trying to figure out.

"They don't really run in the same circles, that's for sure," Patty Sue said, and everyone nodded in agreement.

"Susan was the famed dog trainer, bringing Victory Cup the AKC Dog Show trophy year after year. She was painfully shy though...seemed to spend more time with pets than people," Doris added.

"Maybe that's why she and Victory worked so well together."

Then there was Mike, who started a string of successful businesses all over Savory. From small fishing shops down by the pier to their planned expansion into banking, he was quite the savvy business owner, according to what the ladies had told me. Sometimes, he was called Midas, the man with the golden touch. But a man of the people, he was not. He was quiet and aloof, always forgoing community events and big gatherings. Which was why his huge birthday party had been quite a surprise.

"Winston and Valorie!" Doris exclaimed triumphantly. "That's what they have in common. Mike was good friends with them. Susan worked for them. Surely, they've talked somehow. With all the time Mike spent with the Channings."

The air got charged once more, filled with the question no one wanted to ask. Finally, Rosemary blurted it out. "Do you think...Susan and Mike...were lovers?"

There was an audible intake of air as everyone pondered on this.

"Then why would both of them be dead?" asked Patty Sue. "Because of a scorned lover?"

"Oh, no. Tina Pellegrino is such a sweetheart. She wouldn't hurt a fly!" exclaimed Margie.

"And she wasn't even in the café," I said. "Unless...she hired a secret assassin?"

"That's ridiculous. Plus, Mike and Tina were so in love, you could see it in their eyes, clear as day," said Doris. "Tsk, the poor thing."

Of course, there was Mike's birthday party just a few days ago. Mike in his tux and Tina in her dress. They always seemed to be within an arm's reach of each other, as if they dreaded being apart for even a minute.

"Okay, okay. Scratch that. Let's run through the sequence of events then," I said, redirecting the conversation. "Victory disappears with Susan. Susan was murdered. Maybe she had a feeling something was going to happen to her, so she packed a bag? Unfortunately, the killer got to her first."

"Then we find Victory wandering around the same river where her body was pulled out. Surely that's not a coincidence," added Margie.

"Wait, wait! Have you noticed?" Doris asked suddenly, eyes wide with realization. "Victory was missing for a couple of weeks. But he didn't seem to have lost any weight. A dog on his own for that long would surely be showing off his ribs from the weight loss."

There was silence again, wheels turning in our heads. It was true. Sure, Victory was dirty and grimy, but he still looked well-fed and every bit the show-stopping poodle.

"A domesticated poodle out in the wild? How did he even survive?" Doris pondered, her voice rising in pitch now.

"What are you saying?" asked Patty Sue.

"Someone was caring for him! Victory must have gotten away and gone back to the river!"

Wait, that did make sense. But...who?

"Did they kidnap Susan to get to Victory? Or was it the other way around?"

"If they wanted to make money from Victory, why was there no demand for ransom?" Rosemary interjected.

That also made sense. Ransom was the first motive we had in mind when Victory first disappeared. With bated breath, we waited for news about a ransom demand from the Channings, but it never came.

"Were they simply holding Victory hostage? And Susan was some kind of collateral damage?"

"And then maybe Susan escaped somehow, but the killer caught up to her!"

"Again, why would they hold Victory or Susan hostage without a demand for ransom?"

The flurry of voices made my head hurt even more. Theories were excitedly thrown around, from Russian spies to mafia warlords. But none of it made sense.

"Okay," Doris wheezed out. "I'm officially stumped."

"Two murders. All in the span of a few weeks. And not a lead in sight," Patty Sue muttered, almost deflated.

I thought of Adam and Valorie, the crackle of the radio from the bug, the back of their heads as I trailed behind them, the shards of glass in Adam's hand at the restaurant.

"So, what now?" Rosemary asked, slumping down on the sofa with a poof.

"I don't really know. Mr. B is closing the café for a few days to honor Mike."

I wasn't quite sure how I felt about not having work and a routine for the next few days. Nonetheless, I had a feeling I would be spiraling down the Savory mystery wormhole.

"Well, then," Doris said, perking up. "Perfect time to look for clues."

24

TINA PELLEGRINO

Just barely a week ago, the Pellegrino home was full of life, teeming with celebration and a happy, noisy crowd. Clinks of champagne glasses. Loud laughter. Buzzing chatter. Soulful jazz.

Who would have ever thought that Mike would end up dead?

Now, the Pelligrino house was somber and still. Quiet, save for the murmurs of well-wishers and the shuffling of feet. This time, there was a heavy, subdued cloud filling the air. It was suffocating.

In the middle of the living room, right where the jazz band played, stood Mike Pellegrino's coffin, elegantly crafted dark mahogany gleaming under the chandelier. The wood glimmered under the light, solid and sturdy. Flower arrangements circled around it, the fragrant white roses and wreaths of lilies perched like soldiers guarding the coffin.

"Tina, sweetheart. We're so sorry," murmured Doris. She pulled the grieving woman in for a hug. Tina fell against her, barely able to remain standing.

"Thank you, Doris. Thank you. All of you. For coming." Tina's voice was nothing more than a cracked whisper. Her eyes were red and sunken, her already thin frame swallowed by her ill-fitting black dress.

"We're here for you, honey," whispered Patty Sue, rubbing her back.

"We made you a little something. Now I know it's not much. But in difficult times like these, eating will be the last thing on your mind. So...we thought we'd cook for you."

Margie handed her a large glass Tupperware container filled with the jambalaya we cooked last night.

Crowded in Margie's kitchen, I manned the stove and did the stirring while the rest of the Delta Queens threw in ingredients into the large metal pot. There were enough onions and celery and andouille-sautéed shrimp in there to feed an entire army. And enough Cajun spices to tickle every nerve ending in my body.

"They're practically millionaires," Rosemary had said that night. "They could order a hundred bowls of jambalaya." Still, that didn't stop her from sneaking in a taste now and then.

"There's nothing like homemade food to comfort the soul, Rosie. Nothing like it," said Margie, her chest puffed out in pride. It was her grandma's recipe passed down from generations, almost as sacred as religion itself.

When all was said and done, and our mouths got a taste of the zesty Cajun flavors, Margie gave a slight nod of her head in approval. "Yep, you can feel the love in there. In every grain of rice."

"Okay, I have to admit. It's pretty darn good," Rosemary garbled, her mouth still full of jambalaya. "Tina will love this."

"Oh!" Tina's eyes lit up a little at the sight of the Tupperware. "Thank you. This is truly very kind of you."

"How are you holding up? I can't even imagine," said Patty Sue, rubbing at her shoulders and leading her to the large sofa set in the living room.

"It's been...you know," Tina breathed out, voice shaky like she'd been trying to hold her tears back for hours.

"I...I can't believe it. I...he was just...here," she blubbered, letting the tears free, letting her face fall to her palms like it suddenly had become too heavy. "Before he left, I asked him to buy me a scone from the Crabby Clam. And he said, 'Sure thing' and gave me a kiss goodbye. And that...that was it. Those were his last words to me."

We kept quiet and kept our heads down. Because what else was there to say? The silence was punctuated by Patty Sue's hand rubbing at Tina's back, the fabric shuffling beneath her palm.

Tina blew her nose on a tissue and then got this far-off look on her face like there was something she wanted to say but didn't really know how to say it.

"The preliminary toxicology report..." she started, slowly, voice wavering like a flag in the wind, "the doctor says they are running a full autopsy but the initial tests showed there was something...he thinks it was an overdose."

Her voice was a soft whisper but also low and gravelly. We had to lean forward and strain our ears to make it out.

Did she say...overdose?

"Overdose?" Rosemary repeated. "Well, that can't be right."

Doris nudged her with an elbow to the rib, not wanting to offend Tina.

"I...I meant...I thought it was a heart attack?"

"I thought so too. And I thought that made sense. At first, at least. But...it didn't. Not really. Because Mikey never had a thing for all that fried junk. He was healthy as a horse. He actually just had his annual physical a few months ago, and the doctor gave him a good bill of health."

Just as I thought. But an overdose? This case just kept getting harder and harder to solve, like a thousand-piece jigsaw puzzle with more and more pieces getting thrown out.

"But...overdose? What—" Doris started at the same time I spoke up.

"What kind of drug was it? If you don't mind me asking," I inquired.

"Oh no, not at all. I didn't understand much of the report, and the police over at the station didn't really explain it to me. But there was mention of...um, I think the name was Digoxin," she said, eyebrows furrowing in concentration. "Do you know it?"

Digoxin. Of course. Medicine used to treat arrhythmias or irregular heartbeats. It was readily absorbed into the gastrointestinal tract and acted quickly upon the heart. Too much of it could trigger fatal arrhythmias.

"I've...um, read about it," I lied through my teeth. Years in the homicide division gave me quite the education on toxicology and certain drugs. But they didn't need to know that.

"It's medicine, really, for people with heart problems. But an overdose of it can cause...can cause death," I said slowly. "But I thought you mentioned that Mike didn't have any health issues?"

"Was Mike taking that medication?" Doris asked, whipping her head to Tina.

"No. He wasn't taking any medication. Which is why the police now suspect that Mike was poisoned."

"What? Poisoned?" My back stiffened as the ladies and I looked at each other, the next question swirling through all our minds.

"But who would want to harm Mike?" Doris cautiously probed.

"There's no one I can think of," Tina answered, blowing her nose on the tissue again. "I mean, I know we're not the most active people in the community, but we've never angered anyone! We haven't done anything wrong. Haven't cheated anyone out of anything. We're just trying to live our lives here. I...I don't know. I can't figure it out either," she said, the frustration leaking out of her voice.

"That's true. I can't think of anyone who has a problem with Mike," Patty Sue muttered.

But somehow, Digoxin got into his bloodstream. How? And most importantly, why? Why, why, why? It ran over and over in my head like a broken record.

"Who? Who would even do this?" Tina burst into tears again, and I felt bad for saying something. But it was the truth, and she needed to know that Mike's death was no accident.

"Mikey, he...he didn't really like dealing with people, you know?" she sniffed. "That's why he always hired people to run the businesses. But he wanted to try. Wanted to be a part of the community. That's why he threw the party."

"Oh, Tina dear, I'm so sorry." It was Margie this time, sitting close to Tina and letting her head fall to her shoulder.

"And...and he was only days away from closing that business deal with Winston, you know? The contracts were already drawn up and everything. He was so excited too."

Something about that made my ear prick. Did that have something to do with the murder? It was hard to tell. And what was the connection with Susan? Mike was a business-man; everyone knew that. Sure, he was aloof at times, but he never clashed horns with anyone.

Not that we knew of, anyway.

25

AWKWARD ENCOUNTER

The Alabama heat was a little more forgiving today. Bright and warm without the suffocating humidity. The breeze was sparse but cool, wind whipping through my hair and through Mister's floppy ears.

"Great day for a walk, huh, Mister?" I told him, hand on his leash as he led me through the park.

As if he could understand what I was saying, he turned his head to me, tongue out and wagging, his version of a smile.

The park was nearly empty. We had been walking for almost an hour, and the only people we passed were an elderly couple feeding the ducks and a couple of early joggers breathing in the fresh morning air.

Mister's favorite part was the large pond, stretching out as far as the eye could see. The tall trees reflected on it, creating a mirror effect despite the murky brown water tinted with green. He could spend all day just sniffing the purple lilies on the embankment, then he'd roll around the freshly cut green grass and yip at the poor ducks.

We turned and walked up the hiking trail that led into the woods in relative silence, just soaking it all in. The well-worn path quietly absorbed our steps. A slight breeze rustled the trees above us. The musky, earthy scent of the pines filled my nose. It smelled of hot summers and quiet picnics and happiness.

"This is pretty great, huh, Mister?"

Instead of his usual response, Mister's ears suddenly perked up, tail stiffening straight, his little brown nose wiggling so hard, I was afraid it might leap off his snout.

"What, what? What is it?"

His neck leaned forward, trying to surge toward something in the distance. He strained against his leash like he wanted to take off, and I was the only one getting in his way.

He broke into an excited semi-run, at least, as much as he could with me pulling him back. He kept going, pulling us forward while I tried to grip even tighter on his cheap, nylon leash.

"Wait, wait! What is it? Where are you going?"

I pulled and pulled at the leash. *Damn, this dog is strong.*

"Mister, calm down! If you get lost in here, how in the world am I going to find you?"

He didn't listen. Because, of course not. He just kept on going, his paws nearly digging into the soft earth as he tried to run away.

And then—

Snap went the red leash.

Mister broke off into a frenzied run, arms and legs flailing around like he was a prisoner who just escaped.

"Mister! Mister!" I yelled at him, running hot on his tail. "What is wrong with you? Wait!"

He sped off, quickly disappearing down the dusty trail that led into another wooded area.

"Mister! Come back here! You are going to be in big trouble, young man!"

I ran after him, thighs burning from the sudden exertion.

I wasn't prepared for a workout today.

"Mister! Get back he—"

With the way I screeched to a sudden stop, I imagined that I looked like a cartoon. I managed to catch myself before falling on my face. But my jaw dropped to my chest in surprise.

Because there was Mister.

And there was Jake, down on one knee, petting Mister's head, grinning at him like a kid on Christmas morning. The dog nuzzled his face into Jake's hand, clearly loving the attention.

"Jake," I huffed, still catching my breath.

I glared at Mister, who was now staring at me with those big, innocent eyes.

Traitor.

"You need a better leash," Jake said when he saw me.

He was wearing a cut-off T-shirt and a pair of jogging shorts, his face shiny with sweat. *I didn't know he jogged.*

He was still looking at me, flecks of blue swirling in his eyes, like sunlight glimmering on the ocean. So easy to get lost in. So easy to drown.

Oh, right. He said something to me. Open your mouth, Piper. And talk.

"Yes, right. I'll be sure to buy a new one," I said quickly.

"I just ate a hot dog. He probably likes the smell. You've got a good nose, buddy," Jake said, still rubbing at the soft fur on Mister's head.

"Ah, yes. Hot dogs are...amazing."

Hot dogs are amazing? Oh my gosh, Piper!

His eyes crinkled slightly, and I could tell he wanted to smile. But he didn't.

"Alright. Well..." he trailed off, standing up and dusting off the dirt from his knees.

There was a war raging in his eyes. I could see it. He wanted to turn on his heel and walk away, stop this conversation right in its tracks. But somehow, his foot was still planted firmly on the ground, unmoving.

And then, before I lost my nerve, I blurted out, "Jake, can we talk?"

"About what?"

The softness in his eyes was gone in an instant, replaced by a curt kind of coldness.

Should I tell him?

A burst of bravery ran through me like a live wire. I could tell him! Surely, he would understand. He was a seasoned law enforcement officer. He knew what it was like. He knew the things I had to do for this job. He probably came across people like me before, detectives working out in the field. What I was doing wasn't any different from what he was doing. We were on the same side!

"Well?" he said, raising his eyebrow. A challenge. His eyes were nothing but narrow flints now, hard and unchanging, mouth a curled scorn.

"It's just...I'm...."

I wanted to grab at his shirt and pound at his chest. Make him know without having to tell him. The words were there, on the tip of my tongue, just waiting to spill out.

Just tell him already! Tell him you're Piper Sandstone! said one side of my brain, the one that was always red hot and ready for a fight, the one that always got me into trouble.

You know that's a bad idea. It's not going to end well, said the other, more rational part of my brain. *You have to play the long game here, Piper. If you want any chance of getting back to Chicago, you have to watch yourself.*

"I'm...I'm sorry," I finished weakly. "What I did was wrong."

What is wrong with you? What you did was NOT wrong! You were doing the right thing! You were doing your job! Tell him! said my "cop" brain, like a devil pounding at my skull, willing me to take back what I said.

But I didn't. I bit my tongue and stood my ground. And when he didn't say anything else, we just stood there, staring at each other.

His eyes were different this time. Still the ocean, only now brewing with the beginnings of a storm. Fondness mixed with traces of agony.

Jake cleared his throat as if he were getting uncomfortable—like he wanted to just walk away without saying anything else. But he was far too polite for that.

"You should get a better leash," he said again, turning his gaze away from me. He fixed his eyes on the broken red fabric hanging off Mister's collar.

"Yes. Yes, I'll do that," I answered. Because what else was there to say?

"Have a good day," he said, more to Mister than to me.

Then he walked away, disappearing as quickly as we had found him.

26

DIGGING DEEPER

"**M**ister! Stop digging out there! How many times do I have to tell you?"

I was in my living room yelling outside, the rickety door to the backyard left open to let in the rare afternoon breeze.

At the sound of my voice, Mister stopped in his tracks, placed his muddy paws primly in front of him, and then looked at me with those innocent brown eyes, like he had absolutely no idea where that giant hole in the ground came from.

"Yeah, you're not fooling anyone, young man!"

My gaze went back to the cluttered coffee table in front of me, what I'd been staring at for the better part of two hours. I had laid out copies of the autopsy reports, both Susan's full report and Mike's preliminary results. There, too, were clippings from the town newspaper reporting the murders. And grainy CCTV photos released to the press. Maybe if I just kept staring at them, something would leap out at me and help me solve this mystery.

A deep sigh emanated out of me, sounding like the winds of a storm whipping through the trees.

Right in front of me were the clues of the case. The case of Savory's unsavory killer.

Okay, it wasn't the best name. But Rosemary came up with it, and it sort of stuck.

'Not a lead in sight,' echoed Patty Sue's words from a few days ago.

Maybe I needed to take a break. Get something to eat. Take Mister out for a walk in the park since the weather wasn't too bad. Oh, right. Then I remembered, the memory hitting me with shuddering force. Jake.

Scratch that thought.

Just when I had resigned my fate to sitting on my butt for the rest of the evening, something in my bag started ringing, an old-school tone that sounded vaguely familiar.

Oh right. My phone. Technically, Margie's old phone that she gave to me.

Who's calling me? No one calls me.

On the screen was an unknown number. Part of me just wanted to turn it off and stuff it back in my bag. Probably some annoying telemarketer or something. But then again, it could be important. Maybe it was the chief calling since I had given him this number a while back in case of emergencies.

"Hello?"

"Piper!" exclaimed a sweet voice from the other end of the line. "Honey, how are you?"

"Mom?"

"Oh, sweetie. Forgot my voice already?" There was a teasing tone in her voice, and I could almost hear her smile.

"What...how did you get this number?"

"Who do you think my brother is, hmm?" she said, still

teasing. In the background, I could hear the clatter of dishes, the chop-chop-chop of a knife on wood.

Chief Hobbs. Uncle Richard. Uncle Richie Rich—when I was younger, of course.

"He might be some hotshot Chicago PD chief, but I'm still your momma."

"Right. Is everything okay? Are you and Dad okay?"

"We're fine, honey. I just wanted to check in on you. You haven't called once since you moved away from Chicago," she said, a little hurt seeping from her voice. "And I had to go to the ends of the earth just to get your number!"

I smiled and shook my head. Mom could be so over-dramatic.

I never got around to calling because...well, I didn't think I was allowed to. I told my parents I was moving away temporarily, citing some vague training course I had to take for work, somewhere along the outskirts of Virginia. Mom believed me right away, of course. But Dad? I wasn't so sure what he had heard from his high-ranking friends in the police department. I had no idea if he knew about my botched mission back in Chicago. Or if he knew I was in hiding to save my life. With the kind of luck I had, he probably knew everything.

"Oh. Sorry, Mom. It's the...um...the phone signal. It's really patchy here," I fibbed through my teeth, my fingers picking at the paper in front of me, slowly tearing it to pieces.

The truth? I just couldn't stomach a phone call. Not when I had so much unfinished business on my hands. Not when I was soaked in shame and failure, so strong and pungent it might travel through the telephone wires and reach my parent's estate out in Connecticut, where my dad could sniff it out. Use it as ammunition against me.

"Ah well," she said airily, flicking open the stove hob. "How's the training going?"

"It's okay. A bit exhausting." I looked around at the papers in front of me. At least I wasn't lying about that one.

She gave a little tsk, and I already knew where the conversation was going.

"Have you been eating properly? I would bet my right sock that all you eat out there is junk food and that icky boxed mac 'n cheese you love so much. And are you drinking enough water? It's hot out there in Virginia, I think. Give me your address, and I'll send one of these lovely water bottles I got at the farmer's market last Saturday. It's big enough to hold a lot, but you can also bring it with you when you go jogging. And oh! It's got this little straw—"

I couldn't help but blurt out a loud laugh. Because, of course, she would want to send me a water bottle just to make sure I was drinking enough fluids.

"What?"

"You know I can't send you the address. Chicago PD rules and all that," I said. Also, thankfully not a lie.

"Oh fine, fine. Just be sure to take care of yourself, please."

"Yes, Mom. I will."

There was a beat of silence. Somehow, I also knew where the next part of the conversation would go.

And then, like clockwork, "Your father says hello." She said it slowly, tentatively, like she didn't want to spook me.

"Does he?"

"He misses you, Piper."

My fingers stopped in their tracks. And then continued shredding the papers into tiny pieces.

We hadn't talked in a while, Dad and me. Although I wanted to call him. So many times, I almost dialed his cell phone number that I'd memorized by heart. The urge to call him was the strongest when I first got here to Savory—when I had no idea what was going to happen to me. I wanted to hear his voice, wanted him to tell me that everything would be okay.

I even bought a burner phone from the gas station. I went as far as punching in his numbers. But I couldn't press that damned green button. So, I threw it away.

"I know he's hard on you. But it's only because he loves you."

Tears started pressing into the corner of my eye, threatening to grow too heavy and fall out at any second.

Because I knew what he would have said if I had dared to call him then. *You are a disgrace to this family*, in that scary, steely voice of his. *That is not the Sandstone way.*

The first time he said those words to me was when I was fourteen and had failed my Basic Algebra class one semester.

Suddenly, I was a teenager again, hiding myself in my room and studying until the wee hours of the morning until I topped that same class the following semester. When I told him about it, all I got was a curt nod in return.

This time, it was a botched police mission. I could imagine he had a more colorful vocabulary in his arsenal compared to "you are a disgrace." And this wasn't something I could fix by gluing my nose to an algebra textbook.

"Somehow, I doubt that." My voice was both shaky and clear. I thought about just hanging up and hurling the phone away. Maybe throw it into that hole Mister was digging in the backyard.

"Piper, don't be like that," she said, half-huffing and half-sighing, so fed up with always being the middleman.

Don't be like what? Hard-nosed and stubborn? Like him?

I didn't know why she was so surprised. The apple didn't fall very far from the tree now, did it? I do actually have to be this way, you know, I wanted to tell her. I have to be exactly like this.

"I...I have to go now," I said, feeling the tension spread across my shoulders and tighten my muscles. I stared at the scattered papers on the table, remembering everything I had to do, everything I had yet to prove.

If I couldn't win in Chicago, I was going to win in Savory. If not as Piper Sandstone, it would be as Sharon Sanders.

"Okay, okay," Mom sighed in defeat. "It's just...we love you, Piper. Okay?"

"Love you too, Mom."

And before she could say anything else, I jabbed the red button and threw the phone back in my bag. Then, with renewed vigor, I grabbed the papers on the coffee table, studying them again.

I must have missed something. An important clue that's just under my nose. Think, Piper, think! There's got to be something here—

My train of thought was cut off by the ringing sound of my phone. Again. I stared at the vibrating little black box in my bag. Even Mister seemed intrigued.

Two calls in one day? he seemed to say. *My, my. Quite popular, aren't we?*

When I looked at the screen and saw Rosemary's name flashing, I felt a strange sense of relief.

"Hey, Rosemary, everything okay?"

"Yes, and no? Margie's in the hospital."

27

ALARMING DISCOVERY

"What? Oh my God!"

"Okay, first of all, it's not that serious," Rosemary drawled on the phone. "Don't get your panties in a twist."

"What? Then why didn't you start with something like that? Way to scare a girl!"

"Sorry. But we did find her unconscious at her house."

"What?!" I exclaimed into the phone. This conversation with Rosemary was making my head spin even more. "That sounds pretty serious!"

"She was dehydrated. And something about an electric imbalance?"

"Electrolyte imbalance?"

"Bingo! That's the one."

"So, how is she now?"

"Stable. Still asleep, though. The doctors are still running some tests."

Beside me, Mister looked worried too.

"Okay, you know what? I'll be right there."

Fifteen minutes later, I was in a small hospital room that smelled of clean linen and antiseptic. Margie laid in the bed, looking pale and small, nearly swallowed whole by the white sheets.

"Luckily, we had the spare key to her house and found her when we did," Doris said. "We couldn't get a hold of her. We had plans to go check out that new bakery, Sinfully Sweet, that just opened on Main Street."

"And when she wouldn't answer her phone or open the door, we decided to barge in!" Rosemary exclaimed. "Or, you know, use the spare key."

"She was sprawled out on the sofa. Luckily, she didn't fall and hit her head or anything like that," Patty Sue said.

"She was vomiting a lot too. Hence, her lack of fluids," explained Doris.

The door to the room opened, and in came a young doctor in his mid-thirties. He was tall and fit, with a jaw that could cut glass. I didn't need to look at Rosemary to know that her eyes were bugging out of her sockets.

"Oh! Well, hello there, doctor," she purred in an exaggerated Southern accent that made me want to snort.

"Good evening, ladies," he said, oblivious to Rosemary. "Good news, it's nothing too serious. Your friend just had a bad case of food poisoning. We'll be keeping her overnight to check her fluid intake and electrolyte levels. And we'll also be giving her anti-nausea medicine. So, she'll be good as new in a day or two."

"That's wonderful. Thank you, doc," I said before he promptly left.

We looked at Margie's pale form. The machines around her were blinking and beeping in a cacophony of sounds. She had a tube snaking out of her arm and up to an IV bag.

"She looks like she'll be out of it for a while," Doris said slowly.

"The poor thing," Patty Sue hummed.

"On the bright side," Rosemary started. "At least she didn't eat any of that killer gumbo."

There was a beat of silence as we stared at each other, acknowledging the poor choice of words. Then we lost it, breaking into chortles of laughter that made the nurse passing by give us a dirty look.

"Sorry," Doris whispered. "We'll...we'll let her get some rest. Let's go, ladies."

"So, what now?" I asked as we were escorted out of the room by an angry Nurse Ratched.

"I don't kn—"

"Look! A vending machine!" exclaimed Patty Sue, earning another glare from the nurse.

I couldn't blame Patty Sue for getting excited. Vending machines were just fun. This one was gleaming in bright colors, an array of candy bars and chip packets beckoning us from inside.

"I'm getting myself a Snickers," declared Doris, slipping a dollar into the slot and pressing the buttons.

The machine slurped up the dollar bill hungrily, gave a loud mechanical churn...and then wheezed a bit, trying to eject the candy bar.

For a few seconds, we stood there. Waiting for the chocolate bar to be pushed out into the slot below. But it just stayed there, stuck on the edge, not quite able to fall from its little perch.

"Oh, for heaven's sake!"

Rosemary rolled her eyes. "While you ladies do that, I am going to check out Doctor Hottie some more. Toodle-loo.

Don't wait up!" And off she went, sashaying her hips until she disappeared around the corner.

"Vending machines can be such thieves sometimes," Doris huffed.

"Maybe it just needs a good whack," I said, slamming my palm onto its sides. Another nurse glared at us as she walked by.

The machine groaned and creaked some more, and we thought that did it.

Apparently not.

"Maybe we should put in another dollar," Patty Sue said, already taking out her purse and feeding a bill into the machine.

"May as well give it your whole wallet," scoffed Doris.

Another wheeze. Another little choke, the Snickers bar still hanging precariously from the metal spiral that kept it in place. Doris gave the machine a swift kick with her knee. Patty Sue whacked it again while I bear-hugged the thing and gave it a little shake.

At some point, Doris produced a thin piece of wire which she tried to snake through the open slat below.

"Nuts. It just won't fall!"

"Maybe we should give it a rest. If vending machine abuse is a thing—"

"Fine, fine. Let's just go to the cafeteria then. Maybe I'll get my darn Snickers there."

As we walked away, a young man in blue scrubs took our place in front of the machine. No sooner had we taken five steps when we heard a faint little plop.

"Oh score!" he cheered. "Free Snickers!"

28

EPIPHANY

"Well, hello Sharon! To what do I owe this pleasure?" Winston said with a smile, giving me a little hug.

"Hi! I hope you don't mind me barging in like this. I just wanted to check in on you and Victory. See how you guys are holding up."

My slight detour to the Channing estate wasn't particularly planned. With the Crabby Clam Café still closed and with nothing to do, I decided to just drive around, aimless and restless and every other "less" out there. Besides, after the second hour of me pacing back and forth in the living room, Mister rolled his eyes at me and begged me to go somewhere. Well, at least that's what the look on his face seemed to say.

I thought about stopping by to check on Margie now that she was home from the hospital, but I figured she might just want some time to get back into her daily routine. She had only spent a night there, and I was sure the rest of the Delta Queens had kept her company over the last few days.

So, I stopped at the pet shop, the one where I got Mister's

dog food and supplies from. I still had to buy a replacement leash—a stronger one, of course.

And then I got this brilliant idea to jet off to the Channing estate.

To see how Victory was doing. And to offer my condolences. You know, like a normal person.

And maybe...to dig for more clues.

Maybe that one wasn't totally normal, but what the heck, right? Just jump right into it since I needed to do something.

"The little bugger?" Channing chuckled. "He's right back to his old tricks, chewing at my shoes!" His eyes crinkled when he laughed. He was wearing a white polo shirt, a pair of smart trousers, and weird-looking shoes with little spikes at the bottom.

"That's good to hear. And Valorie?"

"She's doing well. Not home at the moment, I'm afraid. She had an important matter to attend to."

I didn't know whether to feel deflated or relieved. On the one hand, Valorie wasn't exactly my biggest fan. She wouldn't be opposed to throwing me out of the house again if it came to it.

But on the other hand, Valorie was a crucial piece to this puzzle I was trying to solve. I just knew it. Her not being here felt weirdly like a missed opportunity.

"Oh, that's okay. I just wanted to see how you two were doing as well. I'm really sorry about what happened. It was terrible."

At that, Winston's face seemed to sag. I almost felt bad for bringing up Mike's death.

"It's not something that's talked about a lot, you know. Losing a friend. I...I didn't know it would feel like this. It's like my arm has been ripped right off."

"And for you to witness it like that...I can't imagine."

"I just wish they would find out who did this," he said, a far-off look dimming his features. He looked both angry and sad, his eyes glassy and mouth a thin, straight line.

Just then, something shiny propped up on the sofa caught my eye. Golf clubs stuffed inside a large leather golf bag.

"Oh! You like to golf?" I probed. That must have been a good distraction because his eyes lit up immediately.

"Oh yes. Every chance I get! All my best business deals have been closed on the golf course."

On the golf course.

Don't go golfing with him.

Susan's note.

Her warning.

"The...golf course?"

"Yes, I play over at the Camellia Country Club. Sharon, are you okay?"

I wasn't quite sure what I looked like at that moment. Probably wide-eyed with my mouth hanging open, all the blood rushing away from my face.

"Hmm? Oh yes, yes. I'm fine. Just...um...got a little light-headed," I managed to blurt out.

Pull yourself together, Piper!

"Do you want me to call someone?"

"Oh no, it's fine. Maybe just low blood sugar. I...yes, I have to go. Right now. Yes," I said, turning on my heel and almost bursting into a run. I caught a glimpse of Winston's confused face.

"Okay, well, thank you for stopping by," he called out from the porch when I reached my car. "Be safe!"

"You too!" I yelled over my shoulder.

And I really, really meant that.

"I'm telling you! It's Winston! Susan was trying to warn Winston!"

"Are you sure?" Doris asked, studying me curiously, staring at my hair that looked like it had been swept up by a tornado. In all fairness, I did look a sight. I practically bolted out of the Channing house and into the Jeep, pressing my foot to the pedal all the way here despite having the top down.

"I just came from there. He had all these golf clubs lying around. I don't know why I never thought of it before! He practically lives on the golf course!"

The Camellia Country Club, an exclusive invitation-only private club located at the outskirts of Savory, along the shores of the majestic Bankhead Lake. It had almost 200 acres of impeccably manicured grass and a mansion of a clubhouse, with an extravagant membership fee to boot.

"And Susan works for Winston and Valorie!" Margie said, snapping her fingers together like she just solved the mystery. "So it makes sense that she would try to warn him."

"Warn him against who? That's the million-dollar question," piped in Patty Sue.

"Adam Kane." I didn't realize that I said it out loud until all four of them looked at me, their eyes widening as the possibilities raced through their minds.

"You really think so?" Margie questioned.

"I mean, we all do. Sharon here just said it out loud," Rosemary affirmed.

"Well, think about it. The bug we planted in Valorie's kitchen? The way he sounded that day Susan's body was found. He was scared!"

"That's all true," came Doris's voice. "But what's his motivation?"

"Okay, I think...he and Valorie are having an affair." My voice was a little shaky when I said it, but I stood my ground. It was uncomfortably quiet for a while.

And then, a sigh from Patty Sue. "I think so too."

"Wait, what? Really?"

"They keep talking about 'their plan,' right? Maybe that plan consists of getting rid of Winston?"

"That, unfortunately, makes sense," Rosemary said. "And you mentioned he was in the Crabby Clam that night Mike got poisoned, right?"

"Yes, he was there. Acting all weird and fidgety." I remembered the glitter of shattered glass on the floor and the white napkin in his hand, tainted with blood.

"What if he was jealous? Of Winston?"

"And...and!" Margie gasped, looking like she might faint. "What if Winston was the person he meant to poison?"

More silence. But this time, the air crackled with energy.

"Okay, that's it. I'm going over to Adam's house," I said, feeling breathless with a weird kind of excitement.

This is it. We'll find clues, solve the mystery, and put Adam Kane and his pretty blonde hair away for good. Put an end to all these murders before he strikes again. And then Jake will believe me, and so will Chief Hobbs. And Dad, too. They'll know. They'll all know what I can do. What exactly I'm capable of. And anyone who dares doubt me will have to think twice.

"Well, hold your horses, sugar-plum," Rosemary said with a smirk. "Because we're coming with you."

29

HALLOWEEN REJECTS

"Alright, we've got walkie-talkies with the earpiece things. Rubber boots and rubber gloves so we don't leave DNA prints," Margie hummed, taking out various paraphernalia from her massive tote bag.

We were in Doris's old Jeep again, gearing up to check out Adam's house for clues. We watched him drive away a few minutes ago, and I knew his schedule well enough to know that he would be gone an hour and a half for lunch.

"And for the piece de resistance, ta-da!" Margie said triumphantly, pulling out plastic masks in the shape of a monkey face, the kind you would find in cheap Halloween stores.

"You have got to be kidding me," groaned Rosemary.

"We need to cover our faces, don't we? It was either that or the rabbit ones. And I don't want us to look like Playboy bunnies!"

"We're looking for clues. Not stealing the Declaration of Independence!" Doris huffed.

"Well, better safe than sorry, I suppose," I said, gingerly

putting on the flimsy mask. It looked like something a preschooler would wear, but at least it would cover our faces. Granted, it would be useless if the police barged in on us, but at least it would shield us from CCTV cameras just in case there were any. I didn't dwell too much on the fact that Jake would likely recognize us anyway. I mean, four older women and one young one—who else could it be?

"Okay, so what's the plan again?" Doris asked, fitting the mask on her face as well.

"I'll pick the lock, and we very, very carefully look for clues in the house."

"That's it? That's the grand plan?"

"We just need to find something incriminating, something that will link Adam to Mike or Susan. He's got something to do with this, I know it," I said with an air of finality that betrayed my nerves.

"Well, if we find something, what do we do?"

"Send an anonymous tip to the police, perhaps?" Margie piped in.

"Yes! Fantastic idea!"

To be completely honest, I really had no idea. All I knew for certain was I wanted to get into Adam's house and finish this once and for all.

"Alright," I said in the steeliest voice I could muster. I put on the rubber boots and gloves, slipped the earpiece in my ear. It was the kind with the wiggly cord, like what bodyguards and the Secret Service wore. I had to admit, it looked pretty cool, if not for the monkey mask and the weird gear. I probably looked like a ridiculous Halloween reject. But whatever. We had a job to do.

"Let's do this, ladies!"

His house was still and quiet, as expected. It was a Colonial Revival bungalow, similar to mine, only bigger. Weeds grew around the perimeter, among the thick bushes, and around the large walnut trees with heavy branches that swayed in the balmy breeze.

I picked the lock with a specially fashioned hairpin, and it easily gave way with a creaky groan. As soon as we tiptoed inside, my mouth fell wide open under the monkey mask.

"Wow, for someone who looks so sophisticated, his house sure is a mess," I heard Rosemary mumble.

It was a fair point. Adam was usually so put together, so well-dressed with his crisp white shirts and shiny Italian loafers, always smelling like fresh, spicy cologne.

His house, on the other hand, was a different story.

The smell of musk permeated the air like a thick marinade. Everything seemed to be upside down, like a hurricane hit and ravaged the house. The living room was a jumble of crushed beer cans, half-filled liquor bottles, and towers of empty pizza boxes. The tiled floor was sticky like it hadn't seen a mop since...well, never. Shirts and trousers were littered around the place like party streamers—over the couch, all over the floor, on the railing of the stairs, even...up there on the cabinets?

How did that happen?

Our rubber boots squeaked against the beige tiles as we tried to navigate the place without disturbing too much, lest Adam notice anything out of place. Although I really, really didn't think that was a possibility considering the state his house was in.

"Wow. What a slob," Patty Sue breathed out.

"Okay, we have to focus," Doris said, visibly shaking her head like she was trying to stop herself from cleaning the whole place up herself. "The note Susan left. It said: don't go golfing with him."

"Susan was trying to warn...someone. Because the killer would strike while they're playing golf?" Patty Sue said, scratching her head.

"What a weird way to murder someone. Was the killer planning to beat them with a golf club out in the middle of the golf course?" Rosemary scoffed.

"Well, we can't discount that. Maybe he's got golf clubs tucked around here somewhere," I said.

I gingerly opened the hallway closet and peered inside. The smell of mothballs and faint bleach invaded my nose.

"Okay, no golf clubs here. Just...old coats. And some cleaning supplies," I reported.

"Cleaning supplies? He's got those? Then why on God's green earth does he not use them?" Rosemary exclaimed while Margie giggled.

"I'll take the bedroom," Patty Sue said, clambering up the stairway, stepping around an errant shirt and discarded pizza box.

"I'll go with you. I'll check out the rest of the upstairs," said Rosemary.

"I'll do the bathroom," offered Doris. I heaved a sigh in relief. If his living room looked like this, then what in the world would his bathroom look like?

"Oh, thank God," said Margie, echoing my sentiment. "I'll check the kitchen. 10-4, 10-4. Do you copy?" she said, speaking into her earpiece microphone, even though we were only a few feet from each other.

"You've been watching too many movies," Doris chuckled at her. Then she steeled herself and took a deep breath. "Okay, I'm going in."

"Copy that. Copy that," Margie said into her mic, her voice crackling into my ear.

"I'll check the rest of the living room," I told Margie, but she had already disappeared into the narrow alcove of the kitchen.

I looked around the disaster that was the living room. Dust coated the surfaces not cluttered with clothes or empty bottles. The smell was pervasive, clinging to me like a second skin. This would qualify for a dump, I think.

Clues. Right. I have to check for clues.

I took a cursory look around, looking for something that I might have missed, hard to do when there was trash everywhere. On the sofa, empty boxes of Chinese take-out. On the coffee table? Crumbs and a mysterious puddle of liquid.

I opened cabinets and drawers, pawing at old video game consoles and broken DVD players. I clawed through his trash. Nothing but old receipts and fungi-infested leftovers. Thank goodness for Margie's intuition on the rubber gloves.

If Adam was the killer, he might have something here that once belonged to Susan. Or to Mike. Maybe a piece of clothing? Some of Susan's accessories, maybe? Something left at the scene of the crime, something he brought home to hide as a memento.

But then again, if he were a smart killer, he would know better than to bring home a clue that could be used against him. And Adam Kane didn't particularly strike me as an idiot. A slob, sure, but not an idiot.

"Kitchen is all clear. Nothing but boxes of cereal and moldy dishes in the sink. Over," came Margie's voice through the earpiece.

"Bedroom is a mess, but nothing in particular that

screams 'I am a killer.' Did you guys find anything?" asked Patty Sue.

"Negative. The bathroom is disgusting, but honestly, I expected worse. Just old bottles of shampoo scattered around," added Doris. "Does the man not know what a mop is? For crying out loud!"

"Maybe he has a basement or a secret lair or something and—oh no!" Margie cried out, her panicked voice staticky in my ear.

"What? What?"

"The garage door! It's...it's opening!"

"What?! It's only been fifteen minutes!"

"Try telling him that! Oh gosh, oh gosh! His car is pulling up!"

"Quick! Hide! Hide! Hide!" hissed Doris into the earpiece. I could hear all of them scrambling, rubber boots shuffling to a hiding spot. I could hear Rosemary and Patty Sue racing back down the stairs like a herd of elephants.

Oh no, oh no, oh no. For Christ's sake, I don't need a repeat with Jake!

I heard the screech of a car slowing to a stop, the groan of the garage door closing. I looked around. Okay, quick. Hiding spot, hiding spot! Think, Piper. Think!

I spotted the door down the hallway. The little closet with the old coats.

Okay, that will do.

I sprinted to the hallway, whipped the door open, and stuffed myself inside, the weird combination of mothballs and antiseptic instantly making my nose itch.

"Sharon, what's your twenty?" came Margie's voice in my ear.

"I'm...I'm in the closet by the living room," I breathed out. "Geez, it smells in here."

It was quiet for a while. Then, the slamming of car doors. And the beep of a lock.

I tried to make myself smaller, tried to hide behind an oversized winter coat. There was so much stuff inside. I had to be careful not to jostle anything or whip myself in the face with a mop handle. With the temperature outside, I was sure they wouldn't be putting their coats in here. Thank goodness for that. I crouched down as far as I could.

"Oh, oh wait. I can peep through the door hole." I whispered into my mic.

There, through the tiny keyhole, I trained my right eye. Just in time too. Because the door to the garage whipped open. And then quickly slammed shut.

Two figures walked inside, shadowy in the dark. With only the faint light from the windows, it was hard to make them out.

Then the light switch flipped on, bathing the room in a white-hot glow.

And there I saw them. Clear as day.

Adam.

And Valorie.

CRAB CAKE CRIMINAL

A Piper Sandstone Savory Mystery Series, Part 5

By: Karen McSpade

30

ESPIONAGE

Adam.
  With Valorie.
Valorie with Adam.

My head started to spin like an old-school film reel on steroids, click-clacking and whirring inside my brain. I thanked my lucky stars that I was already crouched down in case I passed out in the closet and caused a ruckus.

"Let's not go through this again, Adam," Valorie sighed, exasperated. She flung her bag on the narrow entryway table like she'd done it a million times before. The familiarity of it made the hairs on the back of my neck stand up.

"I wouldn't have to...to keep repeating myself if you just listened to me," Adam said through gritted teeth. The tendons in his neck jutted out, straining, his usually fair skin already turning a blotchy red.

They stood face to face by the entryway, breathing hard, glaring at each other so intensely that I thought for a second one of them would spontaneously burst into flames. Even though Valorie was a few inches shorter, she stood tall in defiance, chin held high with her arms crossing her chest. Adam had his hands on his hips like an angry principal, daring a student to defy him.

"Sharon? What's going on?" I could hear Doris say through the earpiece.

"I...I think they're fighting," I whispered slowly, cupping my hand over the microphone.

"Fighting? Fighting about what?"

"Oh, for heaven's sake, Patty Sue. Just let her listen in." Rosemary's voice sputtered in.

I opted not to say anything more. Any noise I made could be our downfall. Which was just as well, really. Because Adam and Valorie started full-on yelling.

"Can't you be patient for once in your damn life?" Valorie's voice was cold and hard, cutting like jagged steel.

"I have been patient! What the hell do you think I'm doing here? You think this is fun for me?"

"You call that patient? Following me around wherever I go? Your stint at the Crabby Clam that night Mike died? You didn't think that might look suspicious?"

"Well, what was I supposed to do? Just sit around while Winston put his hands all over you!" Adam spat at her. His anger rose to a feverous pitch, face growing so red I feared for his health.

Valorie's eyes widened at that, just for a millisecond. Then she heaved a sigh and pinched the bridge of her nose. "I've told you before. I just need a little more time."

"Time for what? Haven't you had enough? Because I sure as hell have!"

Valorie ran her hand through her silky golden blonde hair, looking for all the world like she wanted to pull it out.

"I'll divorce Winston when I'm good and ready! You don't get to tell me when I'm going to do it!"

Divorce Winston?

Put his hands all over you?

The Crabby Clam that night Mike died? It came to me in a frenzied rush. The glass shattering in Adam's hand. Valorie acting weird and fidgety, constantly looking over her shoulder. Winston's arm around her shoulder.

Wait a second.

We were right...they are lovers!

Only lovers fight like that, with the kind of intimate familiarity where they throw their emotions at each other like barbed wire.

Now, they stood, still glaring at each other. The anger in the air started to dissipate as Adam's face morphed into something that resembled muted softness.

He hung his head in resignation and then muttered, "I just...I just don't know what to do anymore."

Valorie's shoulders slumped, then she took another deep breath like she needed to ground herself. "I know, I know. Me too."

Slowly, she wrapped her arms around him and gave him a tight hug. Adam melted into her touch in an instant. And then they were quiet as if they weren't biting each other's heads off just a few minutes ago.

"After they find Susan's killer," Valorie said. It was a muffled whisper against Adam's shoulder, but her voice was clear and sure.

"What?"

"After they find Susan's killer, then I'll...I'll file for divorce."

"Really?" Adam's face split into a grin.

"You know I'd do it right now if I could, but with everything that's been going on..." Valorie trailed off, her hands rubbing at Adam's back in a calming gesture.

"I understand, and I shouldn't have pushed you. I'm sorry," he breathed out.

"It's okay. It's like we're all on edge these past few weeks." Valorie stepped away from the embrace and walked over to the sofa, flopping down on the cluttered cushions.

"I think that's best, waiting until they find Susan's killer. And Mike's too. It's such a tragedy."

"I mean, who would do this? Just some psychopath on a killing spree?"

"I think they're connected somehow," Adam answered, joining her on the couch, his outstretched arm firmly around Valorie. All traces of their shouting match evaporated into thin air.

If I weren't frozen in place, I would have smacked my head in annoyance.

Of course! Why didn't I see it before? All that sneaking around, one of them always not far from the other, all those times I caught them in a car together. I was so caught up in believing they were partners in crime that I didn't see what was in front of me all along!

"Okay, Sharon, we're dying over here. What's going on?" came Doris's echoey voice through my earpiece.

I took a deep breath. "They're not the killers," I whispered into my microphone, hoping the coats in the closet would muffle the sound of my voice. "It's not Mike and Susan who were lovers. It's Adam and Valorie."

There was silence for a while, and I thought my earpiece got cut off, or maybe they just couldn't understand what I said.

And then Margie's awed voice crackled in. "Oh my Lord. Really?"

"I knew it!" Rosemary exclaimed, and I winced at her voice. "There was always something about those two! I was—"

"Ssshh. They're going upstairs." I whispered. Adam and Valorie had gotten up from the couch and were now heading up the stairs.

"Oh, thank heavens. Let's get the hell out of here," whispered Patty Sue.

"Ssshh. Don't move until you hear them at the top of the stairs."

It was quiet for several moments, and then I heard a door upstairs close. From my earpiece, I could hear the ladies' panicked movements—the shuffling of feet, heavy breathing, lots of frantic whispers—and then the sound of a door being gingerly opened and then closed.

"The kitchen door is unlocked, Sharon! Hurry!"

I breathed out a sigh of relief. *The masters of espionage are looking down on us today.*

I quietly opened the closet door and peeked around. *Okay, the coast is clear.* I tiptoed my way to the kitchen and hurried out the door.

"Get your butt over here!" Rosemary growled at me through the earpiece. They were already in the Jeep, revving up the engine. Patty Sue held the door open and was waving me over. I didn't think we would end up in a getaway car situation today, but here we were.

"Go, go, go!" I screeched when I jumped inside.

"Oh, honey, you don't have to tell me twice," Rosemary muttered as she stepped on the pedal. "We're getting out of here like a bat out of hell."

31

MISSING EVIDENCE

"Well?"

"Well, what?"

"What now?"

"What're you looking at me for? I don't have a stinking clue what to do next."

The Delta Queens had been going at it for a while now, occasionally whipping their heads at me, like I could give them the answers.

All I could manage was a weak shrug and a sip of my Earl Grey tea.

It nagged at me, that's for sure. Adam and Valorie. Lovers. But it was clear they weren't the killers. There was no mention of harming Winston or anyone else for that matter. Now it was plain as day, almost humiliatingly so. Maybe my Chicago PD skills were getting rusty.

"We all thought the same thing, you know," Doris said. I was so out of tune with their conversation that I thought she was talking to someone else. But when I looked up, she was looking straight at me, her eyes soft and understanding.

"Stop beating yourself up. We've got a killer to catch."

"Right, right," I said, finally sitting upright from my flopped-out position on the couch. "Looks like it's back to the drawing board for us."

"So, Adam and Valorie are out," Doris murmured, staring at Margie's coffee table that was now littered with newspaper clippings, pictures from the CCTV footage, police reports, and all sorts of mumbo jumbo that we had gathered as evidence. It was a mountain of papers, nearly teetering off the edge of the wooden table. And yet, still no lead.

"You know what?" I said with a sudden burst of energy. "Let's do this right."

I grabbed a newspaper article from the pile and stuck it with tape on the empty wall in front of the sofa. The headline was written in intimidating bold letters. "TRAINER AND PRIZED SHOW DOG MISSING," it said. And then I taped the grainy pictures from the CCTV footage, the ones showing Susan leaving the Channing estate with Victory.

"Okay. So. Susan and Victory. Disappeared without a trace. The CCTV footage only shows them leaving the estate. And then...nothing. The only clue we have is a note in Susan's house warning someone not to go golfing with...another someone."

"And that someone could be Winston," Doris said, taping a picture of Winston from an old newspaper article.

"Right. And then a few weeks later, her body is found floating in the Tombigbee River." I tacked up Susan's autopsy report, along with a yellow post-it note that read "Victory found in the same place."

Before long, all of us were tacking things on the wall, adding post-its here and there. More newspaper articles about Mike's sudden death. His preliminary autopsy report.

Research papers about the Digoxin that killed him. We were sticking in thumbtacks and tying red string around them, trying to connect things together like pieces of a very damning puzzle.

When we were finished, Margie's wall looked like a veritable murder board, like those things used in crime investigation shows. The pile on the coffee table was gone, save for a lone CD. It was the news coverage from the CCTV clip of the Channing estate that night Susan and Victory disappeared.

"Maybe we should give this another watch?" Margie suggested. "You never know."

The camera footage clip was short, barely more than two minutes. At first, it was still, with nothing but the rustle of bushes to indicate that the camera was indeed recording. And then Susan came into the frame, holding tightly onto the leash with Victory in tow.

She wasn't running exactly. More like hurried steps, like she needed to get away from there pronto. And she kept looking over her shoulder, which I always thought was weird.

"What in the heck is she looking at over her shoulder? Looks mighty suspicious if I do say so myself," Rosemary huffed.

"Exactly. It's like she's worried she's going to get caught stealing Victory," Doris chimed in as if she had just read my thoughts.

"And we're back to square one. Why would Susan steal Victory? What's the motive?" I rewound the video clip until the staticky frame came up again on the screen.

It must have taken six replays before I started to notice something more. The strong lock of her jaw. Her rigid steps. The way her hand shook when she looked over her shoulder. The shine of her eyes against the dim light. It didn't appear like the self-satisfied look of a dognapper. Susan looked almost...afraid?

"What if...what if she was running away from someone?"

"Who? And why aren't they in the footage?" Doris asked, her eyes also glued to the screen.

"Maybe they are...if the tape was played further out. Maybe the killer will be revealed."

"So, we need the complete footage," Doris said. It wasn't even a question, just a simple statement.

"That's all well and good, but we can't exactly stroll into the police station evidence room and ask for it," drawled Rosemary.

"Maybe we could break in?" Margie asked with hope beaming in her eyes.

"Right, because that worked out so well when we broke into Adam's house."

Then there was silence as all of us stared at the screen where the video clip was still playing. Our brows were furrowed, eyes crinkling in thought.

But when I turned my head, Doris was smirking.

"Ladies, I may have an idea."

32

A VERY BRITISH DORIS

"Are we sure this is a good idea?" Rosemary rolled her eyes at Doris's reflection in the mirror.

"Well, it beats sitting around and staring at the TV, that's for dang sure." Doris adjusted her scratchy wig and gave a satisfied nod. Her shoulder-length silvery hair was now wrapped up in a bun and covered under a jet-black wig, cut into a stylish inverted bob. She wore oversized, thick-framed sunglasses, a billowy blouse, and cigarette trousers that matched her lean frame.

"You look like a Karen," Patty Sue guffawed.

"Oh, hush. Let's just get to the police station, shall we? I want to do this while I've still got the nerve."

When we got there, I parked a good two blocks away from the station. Call it paranoia, if you will, but I had already gotten this far without another trip to the slammer. I planned to keep it that way.

"Okay, you're all wired and ready to go... I think," Patty Sue told Doris. "We better check it to make sure it works, just to be safe."

"Mike test, mike test," Rosemary blurted into the tiny microphone subtly clipped to the inside of Doris's blouse. Her voice whined and echoed from the bulky radio transmitter we had set up between the front seats of the Jeep. "Yep, it's working!"

"Alright. Let's rock and roll, ladies."

"Good morning, ma'am. What brings you in today?" Luckily, it was Jake.

"I have a possible lead for the Susan Tate murder case," Doris said, affecting a wildly posh British accent. I would have laughed if she weren't so spot on.

"Oh?" he replied with curiosity. I could picture Jake's wide-eyed expression, like a deer in headlights. I also knew he would be trying to act cool.

"I recently heard of Susan's murder on the news. It was all very drab and depressing," Doris drawled, and I saw Rosemary roll her eyes. "But I realized that it happened while I was visiting Savory. I was staying at a local Airbnb near the Channing's estate. You know, that one off Elm Street? Very charming house with the cutest little—"

"Yes, yes. I'm aware of it."

"Right. Well, I saw someone."

"Someone?"

"Well, actually, a man. Running through the woods just before dark."

There was a flurry of sound on the other end as Jake apparently started writing down what British Doris was saying if the scratching noise of pen on paper was any indication.

"I didn't think much of it at the time. But then I heard of Susan's murder and realized it happened on the same night. It was just so...peculiar."

"Peculiar? How exactly?"

"Well, the man was running, but he wasn't wearing jogging clothes. And it was late, well past eight o'clock. It just seemed so odd. That's why I wanted to come in and report it."

There was silence after that, the wheels in Jake's brain turning.

"I saw the news clip," British Doris continued, slowly, carefully, like she was treading on shards of thin ice. "And I'm just curious...was anyone else seen in the footage?"

More silence.

"Maybe...someone was chasing her?"

"No. There was no one, I'm afraid."

"Well, has the footage been viewed further out to the very end? Maybe...maybe he was much further behind her and—"

"We've reviewed the footage closely and didn't see anyone other than Susan," he said brusquely, cutting her off. "Can you describe the person you saw running?"

"No," British Doris said with a sad sigh. "He was running very fast, and I didn't get a close look at him. I just saw him through the window."

"How about his clothes?"

"Clothes?"

"Yes, you mentioned his clothes."

"He was erm...yes, definitely...wearing clothes!"

Jake cleared his throat. "Well, that's good. We can't have strangers running around naked in the dark now, can we?"

"Wow. This is going swell," Rosemary muttered beside me in the Jeep. I felt my back and shoulders stiffen.

"Any features you can recall?" Jake asked.

"Erm...nothing specific. It was getting dark."

"Was he tall? Or short?"

"Erm...tall! No, short! Average! Yes. Quite average." British Doris was stammering. I let out a huge sigh. This was *not* going very well.

"Average," Jake repeated. "How about his build? Was he lean or maybe on the heavier side?"

"Quite...um...medium build, I would think."

"You think? Or you saw?"

"Well...erm, it's hard to tell someone's build for certain when they're dashing through the dark."

"A five-year-old can lie better than her!" Rosemary said, exasperated. "Heck, even Mister could lie better than her."

"She's nervous! She gets all loopy when she's nervous," Patty Sue said from the seat behind us. She was biting at her nails, making loud chewing noises.

"Well, I see." The tone in Jake's voice was a little hard to read. I wasn't sure if he was angry for having his time wasted or if he had already grown used to strangers coming up to him and giving him all sorts of weird leads about this high-profile case.

"You can give us your contact details, and we'll call you if we have any further questions," he said cordially.

The ladies and I simultaneously shook our heads in defeat.

"Well, that's that," Margie huffed. "Think he'll take the bait and look into the footage again?"

I looked up at the rearview mirror and saw Jake ushering British Doris out of the police station. He was in his uniform blues, looking distinguished and confident. They shook hands, and he walked back inside.

"Guess we'll have to wait and see."

33

PEP TALK

"Well, Mister. I've officially run out of ideas." Sure, my voice was a little on the whiny side, but I couldn't bring myself out of the slump I was in. Besides, it was just me and Mister in the house, so there was no fear of judgment.

Mister was looking at me with wide, unblinking eyes and disdain on his face. Clearly, he was bored with my little pity party.

"What am I even doing here?" I was sprawled out on the living room floor, staring at the ceiling, a pathetic lump lying beside the coffee table. I threw Mister's little squeaky ball at him in a lame attempt at playing catch. It landed with a soft thunk and rolled under the kitchen table.

Mister huffed and scurried after it, probably so he could escape my sad monologue.

"I can't even solve this case, Mister! Maybe Jake is right. Maybe I'm just doing more harm than good here."

Two days of staring at our little murder board got us nowhere—no surprise there. No news regarding the CCTV footage, either. We didn't even know if Doris's stunt would persuade Jake to take a closer look at the camera footage. Again, we were in an almighty slump. And this time, it looked like the Dentures and Diamonds Crime Squad might not get out of it anytime soon.

"Maybe I'm not really cut out to be a detective." My voice was loud and shaky, talking more to myself than to Mister. I looked up at the ceiling, at the intricate weave of dark wooden beams. Maybe I could just lay here for the rest of my life, staring at them.

"That's funny. I never took you for a moper," came a voice from the back door by the kitchen.

My eyes grew twice their size. I lay there frozen on the scratchy rug for a second or two. Thoughts of psycho killers were instantly wiped away when I registered what I heard.

A female voice.

A *familiar* female voice.

Of course, being the person that I was, I let out an almighty shriek, sitting up so fast, I nearly sliced my forehead open on the edge of the coffee table.

Because there stood Morgan and Nancy, strolling casually into my living room, the same way they always did back in Chicago. Funny. That felt like a whole other lifetime ago.

And, of course, Mister didn't even bark. Just sniffed at Morgan's shoes and plopped himself down by his feet. Some guard dog.

"You really just leave your back door open like that? This small town has really rubbed off on you, huh?" Morgan was smiling, rubbing at the back of his neck. He hadn't changed one bit. The dark scruff on his face. The wrinkly button down. The crinkly eyes.

"What in the world are you guys doing here?!"

"Came to visit you, of course!" said Nancy, looking out of place in my little bungalow in her high heels and pencil skirt.

"Way to scare a girl!" I half-laughed, half-shrieked. I managed to get on my feet and wrangle them into a tight hug.

"Wait. How did you find me?"

"Pssh. Have you forgotten who you're talking to?" Morgan scoffed. "I'm like a bloodhound. I can track a piece of gum stuck on a shoe. I can follow a scent and—"

"Your mom gave us your number," Nancy cut him off in a bored voice. "And then, yeah. Morgan did the stalker-y tracking stuff."

"Right. Mom."

Of course. Despite living all the way in Connecticut, Mom made sure to add all my work friends on Facebook. And she particularly liked Nancy. She always thought her girly-ness would rub off on me. Guess not.

"Well, come on in and take a seat. Make yourself at home! I'll make you guys a drink. You have to try Savory's special sweet, iced tea."

I grabbed the pitcher I had in my fridge and started pouring the sweet amber liquid into glasses.

"Look at you, so Southern already." Nancy laughed as she walked around the living room, looking at my sparse decorations like she was in the Met.

"How's everything going at the precinct?"

"Ah, well. It's just not the same without you," Morgan said with a dopey look on his face.

"And here I thought you weren't a cheeseball anymore."

"I meant, it's just such a shame that I don't have my coffee lackey anymore."

I laughed at that, a full-on laugh that made me feel lighter than I had in months.

"I've really missed you guys. You have no idea."

I brought the tray with drinks over to the coffee table and joined them on my little couch. A quiet air descended upon us, calm and comforting.

"What about you?" Morgan asked, voice suddenly soft. "Why were you lying on the ground when we came in? Being all dramatic?"

"Oh, you know..." I trailed off. I didn't want to mope and ruin the good time we were having. But Nancy put her hand on top of mine and squeezed.

"It's okay. You can tell us."

"Well." I puffed out a sigh, not quite sure how to compress all the craziness into something logical. So, I started with the one thing I was one hundred percent sure of. "So...there's a killer on the loose in this town."

A beat of silence as Nancy's mouth fell open, not exactly the bit of news she was expecting.

"Excuse me, there's a what now?"

And then it all came out of me like word vomit. Morgan already knew about Susan, but when I told them about Mike's tragic murder, his mouth fell open too.

"This is straight out of an Agatha Christie novel!"

"Yeah, well, except it looks like this case won't be getting solved anytime soon. We're stuck. This killer is good. They know what they're doing."

"So, what are you and the Delta Queens going to do?" Nancy asked.

"I don't know," I said morosely. "We couldn't piece it together. I mean, I thought I'd solved it! It turns out my main suspect is just having an affair with Valorie Channing. He's no killer, though."

"That's it? That's what you were wailing about? That

you're not cut out to be a detective?" Morgan said, looking almost offended.

"Well, can you blame me? Look at me. I got kicked out of Chicago! And now I can't bring down a murderer who's already killed two people! And one of them was killed in public!" Nancy and Morgan had never seen me cry, but it looked like that would be changing soon. My voice was already cracking, tears pinching at the corner of my eyes.

"Oh, honey. Maybe you just need to take a break," Nancy cooed, rubbing at my back.

And that was it. I started blubbering like a toddler, the exhaustion and helplessness of the past few months coming at me like a raging waterfall.

"Yeah. Regroup. Look at things with fresh eyes, you know?" Morgan agreed.

"No, I don't know," I hiccupped through my tears.

"Piper Sandstone, you are the most stubborn person I know," Morgan said with steely determination. "We know you, and we know you don't quit, so you're not going to start now."

"Wow. Is that the best pep talk you can do?" I said, somehow laughing and crying at the same time.

"You don't need a pep talk," Nancy interjected. She grabbed me by the shoulders and glared at me. "You're going to cry your ass off today. You're going to curl into a little ball and feel pathetic all you want."

"Umm...okay?"

"But tomorrow? You're going to pull yourself together. You'll look back on all your clues, and you'll start thinking like Detective Piper Sandstone of Chicago PD, the ultimate badass who tried to bring down a whole damn drug ring."

I gulped at that. My tears seemed to recede, and all I was

left with were these embarrassing hiccups. Nancy was still glaring at me, and Morgan was grinning and nodding his head.

If they could believe in me, then maybe it was worth a shot.

"Yes, ma'am."

34

WHO'S THAT KID?

It was another sleepy day at the Crabby Clam Café. I could hear the soulful blues music wafting through the speakers and the chatter of the Delta Queens in their usual booth. It was calm and comforting, like a warm blanket. In another time, I would have slipped right into their booth and gossiped with them.

Today, however, my body was here, but my mind was elsewhere. Specifically, in Margie's living room in front of that murder board, trying to weave the pieces together, looking for new bits or connections I may have missed. I must have memorized that wall by now. And Nancy's words from yesterday rang like a bell inside my brain.

Think like a detective. Think like Piper Sandstone.

I must have missed something. Something small, perhaps. It was always the little things that tripped up a criminal, wasn't it?

"Order up! Table 2," yelled Carla from the kitchen, ripping me out of my reverie. I grabbed the heaping tray of food and brought it over to the ladies.

"Here you go. Crab cakes for you, Rosemary and Patty Sue. Baked salmon with pesto on filo dough for you, Doris and Margie." They looked over our daily specials like they had just won the grand prize at bingo. Flaky fried crab goodness with just the right amount of crunch. Baked Salmon on top of filo pastry filled with pesto and a slice of fresh tomato. It smelled like seafood heaven.

"Oh, thank goodness. I've been craving this all day!"

"You say that about all the weekly specials, Rosie."

"No one asked you, Patty Sue. Now let's eat!"

They chattered while they ate, even offering me a forkful of the crab cakes. I stood by their booth, laughing at another tale of Rosemary's antics. But still, my mind kept flying off to Margie's living room wall. It was like I had to chase after my brain, make it pay attention.

The bell by the door rang loudly, and we all looked up. It was a lanky young man who looked oddly familiar. He trotted over to Carla by the counter.

"I have a to-go order. Four crab cakes," said the pimpled teenager in that kind of bored voice that always grated at my nerves.

"So anyway..." continued Rosemary. I willed myself to listen, but something about that boy nagged at me. I took another sly look at him, studied the way his suit nearly swallowed his thin frame. When he got his order, he walked away with an arrogant swagger. And then it hit me.

That guy in front of the pet store! The one who nearly ran me over! Of course. And he picked up Richard, too, that night at the Channing estate when we found Victory. Funny. I never did ask the ladies about him.

I looked back at the Delta Queens still chomping on their crab cakes and salmon, oblivious to my musings.

No time like the present, I guess. I slid into their booth and whispered, "Hey, did you guys see that kid who just came in here?"

"The tall young man with the to-go crab cakes?" asked Rosemary between mouthfuls.

"Yes, him. Who is he? You know he nearly ran me over one time?"

"Ran you over! When?" Poor Margie asked, dismayed.

"By the pet store when I was getting supplies for Mister. He pulled into the parking lot and almost hit me. He was in this fancy BMW. It was a few months ago."

"Oh, is that Martha's boy? Or Violet's from bridge club?" asked Patty Sue.

"Martha's boy," Doris answered. "Marty works as a driver for Richard. He's young, but Richard likes giving teenagers job opportunities. Probably because they're cheaper to have on the payroll."

"See? Richard's hot and philanthropic!" Rosemary said, flinging globs of crab cake all over the table in her excitement.

"Hmm. That makes sense. I also saw him pick up Richard at the Channing's house before. You're right. He must have been running errands for him at the pet store."

"Pet store," Doris suddenly hummed, like she was trying to remember something. Instead, she was looking through me, forehead frowning, mind tick-tick-ticking like a clock.

"What is it?"

"Oh, nothing." She shook her head and sighed. "Yes, that must have been it. Running errands for Richard."

35

SHOCKING MEMORY

"Sharon! Sharon, wake up! I've figured it out!" said a loud voice near my ear.

I blinked my eyes slowly. Surely this was a dream. A very, very weird dream. Realistic, though. I was in my bedroom. *Feels so real.* There was a shadowy figure standing by my bed, hissing at me, their warm breath tickling my ear.

Shadowy figure?

Now, wait just a gosh darn minute.

I live alone!

Before I knew it, I was leaping up from my bed like a ninja and grabbing the shadowy figure's arm, pinning it against their back.

"It's me! Doris! Ow! Let go of my arm, will ya?"

"Doris? What in the world are you doing here?" I let go of her arm and turned on the lamp. "I thought you were a thief! Or a psycho killer!"

Thankfully I didn't whip out my gun. Then I'd have a lot of explaining to do.

"I figured it out!" she yelled. She had this manic look on

her face that, quite frankly, scared me as much as the thought of thieves or psychos.

I looked at the alarm clock beside my bed. It read 5:22 am.

"What did you figure out? And couldn't you have figured it out at a normal time?"

"Oh hush, dearie. Then what kind of crime squad would we be? Justice doesn't sleep!"

She grabbed my hand and led me to the living room, where the rest of the Delta Queens were already sitting on the couch and helping themselves to tea.

"She dragged you all out of bed, too, huh?"

"Oh, sweetheart. This is our normal wake-up time," Margie laughed. They were all freshly showered and dressed while I looked like a corpse that just got dragged out of its coffin.

"Sorry about your arm," I said to Doris.

"Oh, don't worry about it. How did you know how to do that anyway?"

I was barely awake enough to lie my way out of this one.

"Erm...from the movies."

"Movies?"

"I... I've been watching a lot of action movies."

"Margie's love of Tom Cruise and Mission Impossible rubbing off on you, huh?"

"Yep. Exactly." Okay, it wasn't the greatest of lies, but it would have to do.

"Well, I hope you don't mind, but we brought the murder board over and hung it on your wall."

I looked on, half asleep, as Doris walked over and plastered a picture of Victory on our murder board wall.

"So," she started. "We know someone was caring for Victory because he hadn't lost any weight."

"Okay?" I honestly had no idea why we had to have a meeting so early. The sun wasn't even up yet. This had better be groundbreaking.

"Well, I remembered that Richard doesn't own any pets!" Doris said excitedly. She was jumping up and down on the balls of her feet. Then she looked at me with an expectant look on her face. All I could muster in response was a look of utter confusion.

"Alright then. What does that have to do with anything?"

"His wife is highly allergic to cats and dogs," said Margie. "There was this one time, I was walking by Big Frog Bayou Park, and I saw her being chased by this tall, really big dog. Looked like Scooby-Doo, that one. It was hilarious! She was freaking out like she was running from a bear. I thought she was afraid of dogs, but apparently, she's just deathly allergic."

"Think about it, Sharon," Doris said to me in a hypnotic voice. "Why would Richard have sent Marty to the pet store that day? Richard doesn't have any pets. And neither does Marty as far as we know."

"He still lives with his mom, and Martha would never allow him to have pets," Margie continued. "She even made Marty give up the cute baby duck he won at the Catholic Church carnival because she knew she'd be the one taking care of it. That poor kid cried his eyes out and made such a scene over that duck."

Despite my sleep-deprived brain, I was starting to make sense of what they were telling me. We never did figure out how Victory didn't lose weight. And he did seem very well taken care of. Could this be the missing piece of the puzzle?

"Well, maybe...maybe Marty went to the pet store because he got himself a fish?"

The Delta Queens raised their eyebrows at me. Okay, that sounded pretty ridiculous.

"Never mind. That kid does not look like someone who would take care of a fish."

"Maybe we should head to the pet store. To see if we can find out if they know something about Marty," Patty Sue suggested. The ladies all nodded their heads excitedly.

"Looks like we're paying them a visit, then," I said. Then I looked out the window at the faint glow of the still-burgeoning sunrise. "At a more reasonable hour, perhaps?"

36

_____

WHAT ARE YOU UP TO?

"You go talk to her!"

"Why me? You go talk to her!"

"No way! Sharon, you do it," Rosemary whispered to me, although her whisper voice was just a few decibels short of a normal person's shout.

"Nuh-uh. I've talked to her before, and she...she scares me a little bit."

The ladies and I were stuck in some weird stalemate, arguing among the shelves of the Fuzzy Wuzzy Furball Pet Store about who was going to approach Angie, the stern-looking proprietor of the establishment.

"Are you folks going to buy something? You do know I can hear you from here, right?" Angie yelled from the counter, and we all winced simultaneously.

Before I knew it, I was being pushed into the front of the store by Doris.

"Go buy something for Mister, and then we'll ease into the questions!"

"Well?" Angie looked even more bored and annoyed than

the last time I was here. Her hair was a messy frizz, and her eyes wanted to droop even as she talked to me.

"Hi. Yes. I'd like some dog food. For my dog."

A beat of silence as she looked me over. I smiled awkwardly.

"Dog food for dogs. Shocker," she drawled. From behind the shelves, I heard Rosemary snort.

I gave a fake little chuckle as she took out canisters of pre-packed dog meals from a nearby shelf.

"Same as last time? For your beagle lab mix?"

"Wait, you remember?"

The first and last time I bought dog food from her was months ago, the same day Marty nearly ran me over. After that, I started buying Mister's dog food from the small grocery store across the street. Not because Angie terrified me. Not at all.

Angie leaned over to me, so close I could smell the minty mouthwash on her breath.

"I remember everything," she whispered to me with wide, unblinking eyes. She looked at me, then kept on staring for what felt like minutes.

I took a step back and fought the urge to shudder. *What is with this lady? Yep. I'm never coming back here again.*

Then she chuckled. And broke into a childish grin. "Just messin' with ya! Lighten up!"

"Oh. Ha. That's...ha...funny," I chuckled weakly. If I had some sort of telepathic powers, I would have been yelling at the ladies to come and save me already. From behind the stocked shelves, I saw Doris's head peeking out.

"Go on! Ask her," Rosemary urged from behind a stack of kitty litter.

Angie's smile disappeared from her face in an instant. She

rolled her eyes and did a little grunt. "What are you lot going on about? Ask me what?"

"Alright, alright. We came here because we wanted to ask you...do you remember seeing this kid here in the store?" I pulled out my loaner phone and showed her a grainy picture of Marty we managed to dig up from his Facebook page. He looked considerably younger in the photo, but the mean sneer was already there.

"Him? Oh, yeah. He came in here once, around three months ago."

Wow. Okay, Angie does remember everything.

"What did he buy? Can you recall?" Doris asked as she stepped out from behind the shelves, the ladies trailing behind her.

"Lots of dog food, that's for sure. Plus supplies to last a whole year. Treats, dog shampoo, the whole nine yards."

"Did he mention if he had any pets of his own?" Patty Sue asked her. "Did he say anything about what all the dog food was for?"

"Oh yes," Angie drawled some more. "We braided each other's hair and chatted for hours while sipping tea."

I felt the ladies collectively roll their eyes.

Then Angie straightened up, sighed, and said, "He just came in here and told me to give him everything a dog needs. 'Price isn't an issue,' he said. He had a big wad of cash in his pocket, and he basically threw it at me. Weird kid, that one. But he dropped a lot of money that day, so what do I care?"

Interesting. Very, very interesting.

"He obviously didn't know what he was doing," Angie continued. "He's probably never taken care of a dog in his entire sorry life! I gave him all the expensive stuff...and he just took it."

"And did he come back after that?" I asked.

"Nope. Just that one time about three months ago."

Three months. The exact same time when Victory disappeared. Doris was right. This might just be the missing piece of the puzzle.

There was an awkward silence in the room. I could practically hear everyone's brains whirling.

"Right," Doris said, nodding primly. "Thank you very much for your help."

As we turned to leave, Angie spoke again. "What are you ladies up to?"

"Oh. Just...research. Yes. We're researching pet buying habits."

"Mm-hmm. Alright then. Good luck with that research," she said with a smirk.

～

Back in the Jeep, we were all thinking hard.

"That was very enlightening," Margie breathed out.

"So that settles it. Marty obviously still doesn't own any pets. Even Angie could tell he didn't have a clue what he was buying. And 'price isn't an issue'? That screams Richard," Rosemary concluded. "Richard must have kept Victory hidden somewhere, and he just sent the kid to pick up supplies so that no one would suspect anything strange."

"But why? Why would Richard kidnap Victory? And poor Susan just got in the way?" My head was starting to hurt again. *This case is going to be the death of me.*

"What if...what if it was Susan they were really after?" Doris said, almost murmuring to herself. "And not Victory?

Susan did leave a note in her house. 'Don't go golfing with him,' the note said."

"Alright. So, we think the note was for Winston. And Susan was warning him not to go golfing with Richard," Rosemary was murmuring and rubbing hard at her forehead until it turned red. "Why? What's Richard going to do? Poison Winston like what happened to Mike?"

At that, Rosemary's voice faltered, and everyone grew silent. Then suddenly, it was like a light bulb clicked on above us.

"Wait a minute," I said. All the wheels in my head were throttling at full speed, connecting the dots. I remembered Mike and Winston's conversation in the café. Something about business and shares and a whole bunch of stuff I didn't understand. And then the announcement during Mike's birthday party and how he was so excited to be part owner. "Mike was going to be part owner of their company! What if...what if Richard didn't like that?"

"And he wants to be the sole business owner! So, he offed Mike. And now he's planning to kill Winston!"

"Of course! When Mike was poisoned, it looked like a heart attack. It looked like he died of natural causes. We only knew better when the autopsy results came in. And by then, the killer got away scot-free."

"Richard got away scot-free."

The car was a jumble of voices now. There was excitement. And a kind of nervousness that came from putting the pieces together that made sense of all this.

And then, panic. It settled between us in nauseating waves, engulfing us in the confined space of the Jeep.

"Susan must have caught onto his plan," Doris said, her voice now a whisper. "And she was going to warn Winston, so

Richard had to do away with her. Then when Mike came into the picture as a third business partner, Richard had to kill him, too, so he would be the company's sole owner once he followed through with his plan to murder Winston."

"It all makes sense now!" I exclaimed. "How did we not see this sooner?" I wanted to laugh. And also cry. All that time staring at those clues, and it was right in front of us all along.

"I can't believe Richard would be so greedy and power-hungry that he would resort to murder," Rosemary said. "What a turn-off!"

More silence as we all stewed in our own thoughts. Then Rosemary spoke again.

"What are we going to do now?"

I turned the key to the Jeep and revved up the engine. "We have to warn Winston. Now."

37

SHANKED, SLICED, AND HOOKED!

"Oh my, what's going on?" said the Channings' young housekeeper, looking like she just saw a ghost. Well, five ghosts. We were all pale and huffy as we rapped on their door.

"Winston!" I managed to gasp out. "Where? We have to... to talk to Winston."

"What in the world? Who died?" came Valorie's voice from the foyer.

"Erm...no one."

Yet.

Of course, I didn't dare say that. Too morbid. Plus, I'd be damned if I let Richard add another dead body to the mix.

Doris cleared her throat and spoke calmly. "Can we please speak to Winston?"

Valorie studied us from head to toe like she was wondering if she should even tell us. Granted, we did look like a proper mess. But we couldn't get the Jeep's cover up, so we raced over here with all the winds of the seven seas blowing in our hair.

"He's gone golfing," she finally said. "With Richard."

"Richard?"

Oh no. Not with Richard. Of all people, not Richard! I could feel the ladies beside me vibrating with nervous energy.

"Yes. Richard. Over at the Camellia Country Club, where they always play. He left half an hour ago." She looked annoyed at first, wondering what this motley crew was doing, messing up her pristine front porch.

But at the sight of our pale faces, her look morphed into one of concern. "What's going on? Has something happened? Is Winston okay?"

There was a long silence. Then I opened my mouth to speak before Valorie completely freaked out. "Yes! Yes, of course! I mean, why wouldn't he be? Erm...please tell him we stopped by."

"What for? Wait!"

"Sorry, we gotta go! Bye!"

Before she could utter another word, we booked it out of there and raced back to the waiting Jeep.

"Step on it, Sharon! We gotta get there before Richard does something!"

"You don't have to tell me twice." My foot hit the gas so hard, the vehicle squealed and flew out of the driveway.

We parked the Jeep and hurried along a cobblestone path toward the Camellia Country Club's clubhouse. It was quiet, save for the chirping of the birds and the whooshing of the massive fountain in front of the building. All around us were perfectly manicured grounds, massive magnolia trees, and abundant yellow pansies.

The clubhouse rested among tall Loblolly pines, with expensive-looking patios and terraces that were bigger than my entire apartment back in Chicago.

"Do we go in?"

"Valorie did say Winston left half an hour ago. They must be out on the green by now."

"Look, a golf cart!" Doris declared. Beside the staff entrance was a clunky metal golf cart parked neatly by the door.

"Well, genius, it's not like we have the keys," drawled Rosemary.

"We don't need 'em, sweetheart," Doris said with a twang. She jumped into the driver's seat and started fiddling with a couple of wires beneath the small steering wheel. With a faint click and then a sputter, the engine purred to life.

"Where in the world did you learn how to do that? I thought I was the only one who knew how to hotwire a vehicle."

"We all have our secrets, dearie," she said with a wink. "Well? Are ya'll gonna hop on or what?"

"Wait, we're really just going to steal a golf cart?" Margie squeaked. When we all piled in without a word, she just hung her head. "Okay, I guess we're stealing a golf cart."

Doris drove the rickety metal cart away from the clubhouse. Despite pressing hard on the pedal, it cruised at a leisurely twelve miles per hour.

"Wow. We'll probably get there by next year."

"Oh hush, Rosie. This is the fastest it can go!"

We glided along the pathways surrounding the immaculately manicured landscape. Every bush was meticulously trimmed, and even the dainty yellow pansies seemed to grow in perfectly spaced intervals. And just when we thought we were already teleported to a different world, the magnificent golf course came into view.

It looked like an oasis, all smooth land and bright green colors. Mature trees lined the edges of the course, and there were a few sand traps visible down the fairway. The first good stretch was flat, and then it moved into gentle slopes down the course. The pristine beauty of the fairway looked like it stretched out all the way into the horizon.

Dozens of middle-aged men were scattered around the course. Some were in pairs, others in groups, all in various stages of their games. Golf carts sailed along the path, zig-zagging across the expansive space. Young caddies carrying large bags trailed after players, silver golf clubs in hand.

No matter how much I squinted, it was hard to tell who was who in the sea of caps and polo shirts. They all wore nearly the same things!

Richard sure knows how to pick a crime scene.

"How in the world do we find them?" Patty Sue groaned. Doris continued driving while we kept looking for them, heads snapping around in all directions.

"Just keep driving around. Surely, we'll see them at some point and—"

Margie was cut off by the sound of the engine stuttering, a faint grinding noise, then a pop.

"Uh-oh!"

The golf cart gave a slight groan and then stopped with an abrupt screech. And then nothing. Doris tried stepping on the pedal, but the cart only sputtered in return.

Oh no! We were stuck in the middle of the fairway. Luckily, everyone was more focused on their game. We weren't wearing anything that resembled golf outfits, and there wasn't a single club or golf ball between the five of us. We looked so out of place we were downright suspicious.

"Now what?!" Rosemary prodded.

I hopped off the golf cart and checked the motor on the backside. It was a tapestry of bright wires and weird electrical circuits.

"Any chance we could just look for them on foot?" I asked, trying to figure out where the battery of the thing was even located.

"Not unless we want to find Winston's dead body next," Doris answered.

Right. It would take us a couple of hours to completely traverse this massive golf course. By then, it might be too late. Dammit.

"It might be a short circuit," said Patty Sue, materializing beside me. She opened a small hidden compartment, revealing even more wires and a large black box fitted snugly inside. That must be the battery.

"Figures. The terminals are loose," she mumbled. She tightened both ends with quick twists of her finger. "Loose terminals don't give adequate power, and they could drain the battery. Hopefully, that should work. Give it a whirl, Doris."

At first, the engine gave an ear-piercing screech and then a quiet rumble.

"Yes! That worked! Let's go!" Doris yelled, and Margie whooped.

"You guys are just full of surprises, aren't you?" I chuckled.

"I had a boyfriend once who was a mechanic," Patty Sue smiled.

"Taught you a thing or two, didn't he?" Rosemary teased

with a wag of her beautiful eyebrows. Patty Sue just rolled her eyes and laughed.

We continued to glide along the fairway. When we reached the third hole, I thought I saw Winston's and Richard's faint silhouettes in the distance. Two figures side by side.

"Over there! I see them!" Rosemary practically shrieked.

The two looked like miniatures from where we were parked, but I could tell it was them. Richard still had this tall, intimidating air about him, even in his golf attire. He was wearing a white long-sleeved polo shirt and black pants. His silver hair shone under the sun.

Winston had on a bright blue shirt and loud tartan golf trousers. Richard said something to him, and Winston threw his head back and laughed. His tan made him look like he was glowing. He seemed genuinely happy. I felt a little pang in my chest.

"Thank God Winston's still okay," Patty Sue sighed in relief. "We still have time to stop Richard. But they're so far away. Can we get any closer?"

"We don't want to risk being seen," said Rosemary.

"Oh! I may have just the thing," Margie announced. Then she rooted around her giant tote bag like some kind of Mary Poppins reincarnate, pulling out four pairs of military-looking binoculars. "Jackpot!"

"Why in the world do you have these in your bag?" Doris was genuinely perplexed, but that didn't stop her from grabbing one and looking through it right away.

"I was a Girl Scout if you must know. And you are welcome. Oh, Sharon, I'm afraid I only brought four, but we can share!"

"Oh, that's okay. I've got something that will work."

I took out my phone and opened the camera app, which I set to video mode. I trained my phone on them and zoomed in. Then I pressed record, just in case.

"Looks like they're just playing," Margie muttered, eyes fixed behind her camouflage-painted binoculars. "Am I missing something?"

Even on my tiny screen, they looked like two good buddies playing a round of golf and drinking beer.

It was Winston's turn to tee off. He took a stance and aligned his feet. Carefully, he turned into a backswing and then rotated, swinging smoothly, sending the ball flying. He headed back to their golf cart with a satisfied nod and took a sip from his beer placed in the cupholder.

Richard trailed after him and then sat behind the wheel. He started the engine, and then they were chugging off.

"Okay, they're moving. I think we can follow, but we can't get too close." Doris started the engine and drove, maneuvering the cart behind thick trees and bushes along the edge of the course.

"Any chance he's just gonna whack him with a golf club? That would be harder for us to stop than a poisoning," surmised Rosemary, eyes still fixed on the binoculars.

"I don't think so. Richard has too much finesse for that. Besides, he wouldn't want to draw attention to himself," Patty Sue replied.

I swallowed down the sudden onslaught of nerves. "Yes, poison sounds more like his style." Slow, quiet, and sinister. I saw it in my mind's eye—how Richard would look when Winston dropped to the ground, crumpling at his feet. He would play the doting buddy. He would scream for help, frantic and desperate. He'd probably cry his eyes out too. Of course, no one in their right mind would suspect him.

It would be a perfect crime.

"If Richard is going to act, he's probably going to do it now. It's not unheard of for someone to have a heart attack while golfing. It would be the ideal coverup," said Margie. "We just have to be patient."

Richard and Winston stopped by their cart and chose their golf clubs. We parked behind a particularly large beech tree, watching and waiting.

Patty Sue looked into her binoculars and sighed. "I hate to say this, but Richard doesn't look like he's up to anything criminal. Maybe they really are just playing golf."

"Well, we can't take any chances," I said. "If nothing happens, then I guess we just watched a game of golf."

I zoomed in a little closer on Richard. He was laughing with Winston, probably some inside joke you can only have with someone you've known a long time. Then he positioned himself by the ball, in a perfect golf stance, spine and knees lined up, golf club firmly in hand. Then he swung, turning his hips and sending the little white ball flying into the air until it disappeared from sight.

I didn't know much about golf, but it seemed like a good shot. He smiled, and Winston gave him a pat on the back. Richard looked like he was having a good time. Would he really murder his friend today? Maybe Rosemary was right. What if we were wrong?

A little bit of chit-chat between the two, a sip of their beer, and then they were back on the golf cart.

"Right, they're moving again."

They progressed through the round, each of them hitting their golf ball with a loud thwack. All the while, we followed and kept watch.

"Okay, I'm not so sure about this anymore. We've been

following them for a while now. They're just drinking beer and playing golf, aka the most boring game in the universe," huffed Rosemary.

"C'mon, Richard. Go on and do something stupid. We've got you now," I muttered under my breath.

"They're teeing up for the sixteenth hole now. Maybe we got it all wrong." This time, it was Doris who spoke. I felt deflated. What if Richard decided to murder Winston when it was just the two of them? And no one would be around to catch him? As much as I was willing to, I couldn't possibly follow Winston wherever he went. Do we just let Richard do whatever he wanted and get away with it?

Just when I was about ready to throw in the towel and suggest we go back, Rosemary shrieked again. She was looking through the binoculars, the color instantly draining from her face.

"Oh, my God! Richard's putting something in his drink!"

All four heads whipped to the screen in my hand. I was so lost in my thoughts that I almost missed it.

Sure enough, there it was. Clear as day. Richard was looking around, slow and sly, checking if he was in the clear. And then, from a small bottle hidden up his sleeve, he poured a clear liquid into Winston's drink. It fizzled up and then stilled until it looked like any normal bottle of chilled, foamy beer.

"Oh my God. He is!"

"Gas it now!" I told Doris. Within seconds, we were out of our hiding spot behind the bushes and sailing toward them on the green. "Margie, call Jake and tell him to get here NOW!"

Winston was looking at something in the distance, probably calculating his next shot. Richard handed him the tainted beer, and he took it without a care in the world, the chilled glass warming under his hand. Their backs were to us, and they didn't seem to hear us approaching. Thank goodness for these stealthy electric carts.

We drew closer until we were twenty yards from where they were standing.

"Sharon, what are you doing?" Doris asked, her voice a shaky whisper.

I didn't have the wits to give an answer anymore. Time seemed to slug into a crawl, like the weird kind of slow-motion you see in the movies. All I saw was Winston slowly bringing the glass of beer to his mouth.

I had already jumped out of the golf cart and was running toward them at full speed, closing the distance.

Richard turned his head, sensing that someone was behind them. But I kept my gaze focused on Winston's back. I pushed hard off my right leg, leaping from the ground. Then, in mid-air, I pivoted my right hip forward and swung my right leg around into an aerial round-house kick that slammed into Winston's back. Hard.

He lurched forward from the contact, falling to his knees, his beer barely touching his lips before he dropped it. The bottle rested on its side, forming a foamy puddle on the bright green grass.

"What the..." Winston sputtered.

I'll apologize later.

Before I could even turn my head to glare at Richard, he took off running.

Oh no, you don't!

I chased after him, gaining on him quickly. When I got within a few feet away, I lunged forward, tackling him to the ground with a loud thump. *Gotcha!*

"What the hell? Get off me!" Richard quickly flipped around on his back, using his legs to try and kick me off.

I pinned my weight on him to hold him down, but his arms were flailing, trying to grab my neck.

"It's over, Richard!"

"Get off me! You're crazy!" He grabbed my hair and pulled. The movement seared at my scalp, but not enough to pull me away from him.

I yanked him toward me, wrapping my right forearm around his neck. And then I squeezed, hard enough to subdue him. He gasped and choked, trying to wrench my arm away from his neck.

"It's over, Richard. We know you did it." I was huffing and puffing, but my voice was clear. "Confess right now, and we'll make it easier for you."

"Never," he wheezed. His face was turning red. He was still squirming from my hold, trying to pull away.

"Sharon!" The deep steely voice nearly made me jump.

I looked up and saw Jake. He was racing toward us, face unreadable. He was in his street clothes, badge hanging from his neck.

"Hold on, let me explain." I knew it didn't look good— Richard and I coiled together like two warring snakes.

"No, wait! Richard was trying to poison Winston!" Rosemary practically yelled, coming to my defense.

"What?" Winston exclaimed, also coming toward us, his shirt stained with beer. "What the hell is going on? What are you doing? Let Richard go!"

"Richard slipped this into Winston's beer." Doris handed Jake the small glass bottle that rolled out of Richard's sleeve when he took off running. "Digoxin. The same substance that was found in Mike's system."

Ha! I knew we were right.

Jake took the small bottle and studied the contents. Luckily, there was a little bit of liquid left inside. He produced a clear plastic bag labeled "evidence" from his pocket and put the bottle inside.

"What is going on? Richard, is this true?" Winston stared at his friend and business partner in utter shock. Richard was still in my chokehold, but he turned his head away, avoiding Winston's gaze.

"We have a video recording of it, too," Doris said, holding up my cell phone. I had handed it to Doris when I jumped out of the golf cart and went all ninja on Richard.

"Yes, I did it," Richard growled under his breath. Then he snapped his head toward Winston. "You don't have what it takes! You were going to run my business into the ground! And Mike? He should've stuck to manning his little lemonade stands. I can make this company successful! Me! And I'd do it all over again!"

I barely heard him over the thumping of my heartbeat. But I did. And it was a good enough confession.

He strained against my hold, his strong arm pulling against mine, a final bid at escape. He grunted and groaned, squirming like a dying fish.

"Richard Price, you have the right to remain silent," said Jake, taking out a pair of handcuffs.

I released Richard from my hold and let Jake take him. "Anything you say can and will be used against you in a court of law. You have the right to an attorney. If you cannot afford an attorney, one will be appointed for you."

Everything moved in slow motion again. Richard defeated, putting his hands behind his back, Jake clicking the handcuffs, Winston looking on in a shocked daze, several police cars gathered on the green grass, flashing their lights.

Jake put Richard in the back of the closest vehicle and walked back over to us.

"Thank you, ladies. The city is grateful for your help," he said earnestly. Then he looked over at Doris and winked. "And I appreciate the anonymous tip from the British lady at the Airbnb.

Doris laughed, and the rest of the ladies giggled. "Anytime, Sheriff."

"Tell her she was right; the killer was revealed at the end of the video footage. So, when Valorie told me that Richard and Winston had gone golfing today and that you ladies peeled out of the driveway to find them, I raced over here."

Before Jake walked off, he turned to me, a grin on his face.

"I don't know much about you, Sharon, except that you are one impressive lady. With a *lot* of explaining to do."

I nodded my head and smiled.

"Soon. I promise. But I may not be as interesting without any secrets."

"Somehow, I seriously doubt that," Jake smiled back with a wink.

EPILOGUE

"Chief Hobbs."

"Piper."

I didn't realize I was holding my breath until I huffed out a shaky exhale. It had been almost a week since "the incident," and Richard's arraignment would be happening soon. I thought I'd get a few days of peace and quiet before all the chaos began, but then I saw Chief Hobbs's name ringing on my screen. So much for peace and quiet.

"Quite a bit of a ruckus down there in Savory, hm?"

He didn't sound mad. More like amused. I figured it was time to come clean, even though it seemed like he knew everything already.

"Right. I know you told me to stay out of trouble—"

"But trouble just keeps finding you, doesn't it?" he chuckled.

I laughed a little at that, relieved that I wouldn't be getting a lecture. Yet.

"Apparently so." I bit my lip, wondering if I should ask about Chicago. *Might as well get everything out in the open.*

"So, any news? About Chicago?"

"Ah yes. That's actually why I called. We're getting closer, Piper. But it's going to be a little while longer."

"Oh. That's...that's great." Unfortunately, my voice sounded flat like cardboard. I wasn't quite sure what to do with that information.

"I know you're bored out of your mind waiting tables at the Crabby Clam Café. But hang in there, kiddo. This will all be over soon, I promise you. I know you're made for much bigger things."

"Thank you, Chief. That means a lot."

"Also, I may have some crime work for you down there in Savory."

That piqued my interest. I gripped the phone tighter to my ear as he continued to talk.

"Of course, you'll have to stay undercover. But I can send down one of our new agents to help you out. She was a former bounty hunter, and she's tough as nails."

I peeked out from the kitchen, where I excused myself to take the phone call. There, on my old couch in the living room, sat the Dentures and Diamonds Crime Squad, happily munching on scones and drinking hot tea.

I couldn't help but smile as I watched them. "You know what? You don't need to send an agent. I have my own team of detectives...and they eat nails for lunch."

"Well, that's great! Listen, I have to get going, but I'll get back to you soon with all the details."

"Got it. Oh, and while I'm thinking of it ... any chance that I can get my Hemi sent down? What's a girl to do without her speed racer?"

Chief's laughter rang through the receiver, "Nice try, Piper. Talk to you soon."

With that, the call ended, but I couldn't tear my eyes away from the Delta Queens. *I* didn't solve this case. *We* did. We found Victory Cup Valentino and caught Richard Price red-handed. These women meant the world to me. They gave me a family when I could have easily been left an outcast. If there's a group of people out there who would never judge me for my past, it would be them. They deserved to know the truth.

Time to come clean.

∿

"Everything okay there, Sharon?" Margie asked as I took my place beside her on the couch.

"Yes, yes. Everything's great."

"That seemed like a pretty serious phone call. Was that your parents?" Rosemary asked between mouthfuls of scone.

My brain started formulating a lie about telemarketers, almost on autopilot. And then it dawned on me that I never really told them anything about my family, real or made up.

"That was...um..."

All four heads stared at me intently, wondering why I couldn't answer a simple question.

"Look, you guys. I have something I have to tell you." I was breathing fast now, and I could tell by the look in their eyes they were getting more and more worried by the second.

"Oh my Lord! Are you pregnant?" Rosemary shrieked. Margie's eyes widened, and Doris elbowed her in the ribs.

"Goodness, no. It's just...there's something I've been keeping from you guys, and I think it's time you should know."

They all stared at me with ridiculously unblinking eyes. If

I wasn't so nervous about telling them, I would have snapped a picture of their faces.

"My name's not really Sharon. It's Piper. Piper Sandstone."

A beat of silence. They still hadn't blinked.

"And I'm an undercover detective for the Chicago PD."

"Excuse me, you're a what now?" Rosemary said. I felt myself wince. *Oh no, what if they hate liars? What if they ban me, cast me out of the group, and kick me out of Savory? Great. Kicked out of Chicago and kicked out of Savory. Everyone's just going to kick me out.*

And then, Margie squealed, her face breaking into a wide grin. "Undercover? Oh my! Like Ethan Hunt?" My shoulders sagged in relief a little bit. It was just par for the course, really, good ol' Margie and her action movies.

"That's quite a lot of information to take in," Patty Sue said in a daze.

"Is this like one of those pranking shows?" Rosemary asked. "Is there a hidden camera in here right now?"

Doris was just chuckling and shaking her head. "I knew it!"

It was my turn to stare at Doris. "Wait, you knew?"

"I knew something was up with you when you pulled all those ninja martial arts moves out of nowhere! Remember when I woke you up that morning, and you nearly put me in a chokehold?"

"Oh yes. That." That move I pulled on Doris. I smiled at her, all sheepish. "Sorry about that."

"And the way you tackled Richard to the ground and put a hold on him that had him squirming like a baby! You never told us anything about where you came from. You just popped up out of nowhere!" Doris was full-on laughing now, and I felt a weight lift from my chest.

"I did always wonder how you knew how to pick locks," Patty Sue added.

"That's why you were so invested in the case! You're just a natural blood-hound detective!"

"And you knew all that stuff about the listening bugs! You set it up like you've been doing it for years!"

They started talking over each other then, laying out their own clues and observations like I was another case that had been solved.

"But why are you here, Sharon? Don't get me wrong, it's not that I don't want you here. I just don't get why a high-flying city detective like you would end up here in Savory?" Doris asked.

And then I told them everything. The drug ring. The corrupt cops. The gala where I busted their faces. How the Chief banished me here to keep me safe. All the while, they just listened intently and nodded their heads in understanding.

"I'm sorry I didn't tell you sooner. I thought you guys would be mad."

"Why would we be mad?" asked Patty Sue, incredulous. "Sure, you gave us a different name, but I'd like to think we got to know the real you."

I looked around at their smiling faces and felt the endless warmth they had brought me. Patty Sue couldn't have been more right. Thank heavens for that.

"I propose we make a toast," Doris said, lifting her cup of tea into the air, "to Piper Sandstone, our new honorary member of the Dentures and Diamonds Crime Squad. May she help us keep the streets of Savory safe while we're lucky enough to have her here!"

"To Piper!" they cheered in unison to the clinking of our tea mugs.

"Hey, Piper."

"Yeah, Margie."

"Do you think you could teach us one of those fancy chokehold moves?"

"Anything for you, Ethan," I said with a wink as we all burst into laughter.

When I went up to Jake at the police station asking to talk, a part of me thought he would brush me off like lint. Instead, he gave a slight nod in agreement. "Meet me at the Crabby Clam on Tuesday for lunch. I know it's your day off." Then he walked away before I could say anything else.

"Thanks for meeting up with me," I told Jake as I slid into the booth across from him. The Crabby Clam Café was already full of lunchtime patrons, and today I was just another customer. I felt myself take a deep breath in and hold it before I let out a sigh of relief.

"Like I said, you have a lot of explaining to do," he answered back, not taking his eyes off the menu.

"Right. No point in beating around the bush."

"Let's start with something simple. Like your name." He closed the menu and looked at me, his face cold and calculating like he was waiting for me to trip up and lie. "I know it's not Sharon Sanders. I ran your name and social security number on the nationwide system. There was no match."

"Piper," I said, meeting his gaze straight on. "My name is

Piper Sandstone. And I'm an undercover detective for the Chicago PD."

"Hmm, okay." I couldn't tell if he was impressed or annoyed. "And why are you here?"

I recounted my story again, the same way I did for the Delta Queens. But while they just sat and listened, Jake hit me with a barrage of questions.

"Wait, wait. Let me get this straight. That mission of yours at the gala. It was just to collect intel, right?"

"Right." I knew where this was going.

"But you pounced on those dirty cops without permission from your superior?"

Leave it to Jake to give me a lecture on the intricacies of police work.

"I know, I know. I was looking for trouble," I sighed. "But I just couldn't stand by and do nothing!"

"Hell, trouble is your middle name," he laughed, and I felt myself relax a bit. "This explains so much about you."

"About me?"

"Yeah. Explains why you're so stubborn!"

"Well, you're the same way!" I was just teasing, but before I could catch what I said, it had already slipped out of my mouth.

"Yeah, I guess we are cut from the same cloth," he said with a smile.

"Touché," I laughed back.

I wanted to stay in that moment, where the conversation was light, and we were just making fun of each other. But I knew I had to get the uncomfortable apologies out of the way. "Listen, I'm truly sorry. About everything I did. I know I was out of line."

He nodded and averted his gaze a little. "What you did

was out of line. And a detective like yourself? You should have known better." And there it was. The lecture. But I knew I had to take it.

"But..." he trailed off, rubbing the dark stubble on his chin. "You did catch the killer. You saved Winston, and who knows how many others. You saw things we didn't, and we are very grateful. I am grateful."

His face was bright and earnest, with no trace of the anger from weeks ago.

"So, what happens now? Are you going back to Chicago?"

"No, it's still not safe for me to go home."

Months ago, it would have pained me to say those words. I would have crawled back to Chicago on all fours if I could. Now, though? It didn't seem so bad. If anything, Savory was pretty darn great. I looked around the crowded Crabby Clam Café, at the chaos that had started to feel like home, at the Delta Queens in their booth dying to know what Jake and I were talking about.

"So, you're staying." It wasn't a question, just a plain state-ment. Jake had that sly little smirk on his face.

"I'm staying. Will that be a problem, Sheriff?" I hit him back with a smile of my own.

"No, we need someone like you around here, Piper Sandstone."

THE END

When an art heist ends in murder, can Piper and her senior crime-fighting gal pals catch the killer before she

gets marked off the hit list? Find out in the next thrilling, hilarious, and heartwarming mystery adventure. If you enjoyed these quirky fun characters and spending time down in Savory, Alabama, I've got something very special in store for you in the second Piper Sandstone series!

Use the QR code below to snag your copy of Bacon, Bodyguards, and Ballistics and dive into the next deliciously thrilling whodunit!

Don't miss the next hilarious and thrilling Piper Sandstone adventure in Savory, Alabama. **Snag your copy of Bacon, Bodyguards, and Ballistics** using the QR code below and get ready to devour a deep fried revenge murder mystery!

She's a Chicago detective hiding in a seaside town with a lot to prove...and everything to lose.

Reeling with excitement over the opening of a private

investigation agency and her budding romance with the sher-iff, Piper Sandstone can't wait to launch her dream career and return to a somewhat normal life. But danger lurks on the horizon—the dirty cops back in Chicago still want her dead. They are ruthless and on the hunt; no price is too steep for her head.

But Piper's already in a predicament of prodigious proportions when an art heist at the Bancroft Estates leaves a bodyguard dead... and she and her crime-fighting gal pals are at the center of the crime scene. With more suspects than the hottie sheriff can shake a stick at, it's no surprise the Mayor has requested help from the new private eyes.

Tangled in another mystery in Savory, Alabama, Piper is determined to solve the case with the help of her quirky senior sleuth friends dubbed the Dentures and Diamonds Crime Squad. These zany retirees traded in their female rock band glory to fight crime, but can they help Piper maintain her cover and catch the killer before she or another Savory resident winds up dead?

Use the QR code to snag your copy of Bacon, Body-guards, and Ballistics and get ready to devour a deliciously fun and thrilling cozy mystery that is unputdownable! Recipes included.

SNEAK PEEK

Bacon, Bodyguards, and Ballistics
From the Prologue

It was a bright winter day in Savory, Alabama, but in Mayor Alice Townsend's office, a heavy, gray cloud loomed above us. She was gnawing at her nails and pacing back and forth until her chunky heels left imprints on the blue carpet.

"We are in the middle of a PR nightmare in this town," Mayor Townsend stated the obvious as she shook her finger high above her head. "Savory, Alabama is supposed to be a cozy town. Quiet. Safe. The kind of sleepy little coastal place you want to bring your family to for vacation." I looked her straight in the eyes and nodded quietly in agreement.

"You know what it's NOT?" Her bright green eyes were wide and manic, hands flip-flopping in the air. "A hotspot for murders and serial killers!"

I stood rooted to the spot in front of her desk. Beside me was Jake, the tough-guy sheriff of the aforementioned cozy little town. It felt like high school again, and we were taking a tongue-lashing in the principal's office. Only Alice was much prettier to look at, even with her anxious nail-biting and huffing.

Being the bearer of bad news was never fun or easy, but somebody had to do it, and today that somebody happened to be us.

"I mean, didn't we have enough last summer?" she said, falling to her chair with a tired groan. "Poor Marco Jenkins. I've known his family since they were kids."

Marco Jenkins. The subject of said bad news. Early twenties. Savory born and raised. Worked as a security guard on one of the estates near town. A quiet kid, from what I'd heard. Kept his head down and his nose clean.

So, it was quite the shock when a poor mailman found his body floating in Cold Stone Creek. With a knife firmly lodged in his back.

"An investigation is underway, Mayor," Jake piped up. "I assure you, we'll be—"

"Jake, the Queen Bee's Private Eyes will be working with the sheriff's department to solve this case," the mayor said before turning her head to me. "That's why I called you here today, Sharon."

"What? You can't be serious, Mayor!"

"Hey!"

"No offense, but it's far too dangerous. We don't really know what we're dealing with here."

"Exactly," the mayor said without missing a beat. "We need all the help we can get. And the Delta Queens—and Sharon, too, of course—certainly stepped up last summer."

I gave her a proud, wide grin but then toned it down when I remembered we were dealing with a murder. Again.

"Fine," Jake resigned. "But you better do exactly as we say."

"I make no promises," I said with a smirk. He bristled slightly but then shook his head with a faint smile.

"We need to know all the details," I said, taking out my notepad and getting straight to business. "Who was he last with?"

Jake's blue eyes turned icy, his face sour like he just remembered something terrible. "CCTV footage showed him leaving a bar with his twin brother."

"His twin?" Mayor Alice stopped gnawing at her nails as her big eyes widened even further. "You mean Max?"

Jake's nod was grim.

"Yes, Max. And we have reason to believe that he murdered his brother."

Snag your copy of Bacon, Bodyguards, and Ballistics here and get ready to devour a deliciously fun and thrilling cozy mystery that is unputdownable! Recipes included.

RECIPES

Savory Shrimp & Grits

If you live in the South, you've probably enjoyed some variety of grits in your lifetime, and if you're lucky enough to live near a fresh seafood source, you've probably even tried one of my family's favorite dishes, shrimp and grits. What makes this dish so rich and distinctive is the roux—the magic is in the roux!

This dish was one of my inspirations for the Savory Murder Mystery Series, so I would be remiss if I didn't share my favorite shrimp and grits recipe with you! I stumbled across this one while perusing Allrecipes.com and modified it to meet my own personal tastes. You can search their site for "Old Charleston Style Shrimp & Grits" to see Berskine's version.

Ingredients: Makes 8 servings

- 3 cups water
  - 2 teaspoons salt

- 1 cup coarsely ground grits
- 2 cups half-and-half
- 2 pounds uncooked shrimp, peeled and deveined
- salt to taste
- 1 pinch cayenne pepper, or to taste
- 1 lemon, juiced
- 1 pound andouille sausage, cut into 1/4-inch slices
- 5 slices bacon
- 1 medium green bell pepper, chopped
- 1 medium red bell pepper, chopped
- 1 medium yellow bell pepper, chopped
- 1 cup chopped onion
- 1 teaspoon minced garlic
- ¼ cup butter
- ¼ cup all-purpose flour
- 1 cup chicken broth
- 1 tablespoon Worcestershire sauce
- 1 cup shredded sharp Cheddar cheese

Directions:

1. Bring water and 2 teaspoons of salt to a boil in a heavy saucepan over medium-high heat. Whisk grits into the boiling water, and then whisk in half-and-half. Reduce heat to medium-low and simmer, stirring occasionally, until grits are thickened and tender, 15 to 20 minutes. Set aside and keep warm.
2. Sprinkle shrimp with salt and cayenne pepper to taste. Add lemon juice, toss to combine, and set aside to marinate.

3. Place sausage slices in a large skillet over medium-high heat. Cook, stirring occasionally, until browned, 5 to 8 minutes. Remove sausage from the skillet.

4. Add bacon to the same skillet and increase heat to medium-high. Cook until evenly browned, about 5 minutes per side. Transfer bacon to paper towels to drain, then chop or crumble when cool enough to handle. Leave bacon drippings in the skillet.

5. Add bell peppers, onion, and garlic to the bacon drippings; cook and stir until onion is translucent, about 6 minutes.

6. Stir cooked sausage and marinated shrimp into the skillet with the cooked vegetables. Turn off the heat and set aside.

7. Melt butter in a small saucepan over medium heat. Whisk in flour, stirring to create a smooth roux. Turn heat to low and cook, stirring constantly, until mixture is golden brown in color, 8 to 10 minutes. Watch carefully, the mixture burns easily.

8. Pour the roux over the sausage, shrimp, and vegetables. Place the skillet over medium heat, add chicken broth, bacon, and Worcestershire sauce, and stir to combine. Cook until sauce thickens up and shrimp turn opaque and bright pink, about 8 minutes.

9. Just before serving, mix sharp Cheddar cheese into grits until melted, and grits are creamy and light yellow. Serve shrimp mixture over cheese grits.

*Original recipe is from Allrecipes.com | by Berskine | Old Charleston Style Shrimp & Grits

Pizza by the Sea

Seafood pizza lovers unite! This recipe brings two of my favorite foods together in a delicious savory blend that uses pesto for the base of the pizza. I created this easy recipe one night when I was experimenting in the kitchen.

Then I decided to test it on company to see if I had really created a dish worth the hype. It received 5 stars each time I served it, so I decided to include this recipe in the Savory Mystery Series. The fresh ingredients mixed with the seafood and pesto sauce make this a delicious and memorable dish. Serve with a salad and dinner is ready!

Ingredients: Makes 1 12" inch pizza; double this for 2 pies
- 1 12" pre-made pizza crust (hand tossed or thicker crust)
- ¾ cup raw shrimp (medium) cut into small pieces
- ¾ cup raw white fish (cod, tilapia or halibut) cut into small pieces
- ½ cup smoked Salmon cut into small pieces
- 1 cup fresh spinach
- ½ cup fresh mushrooms diced
- ¼ cup grape tomatoes diced
- 1 cup of Italian 4-cheese blend
- 4 tablespoons of pesto sauce
- 2 tablespoons of butter
- Salt and pepper to taste

Directions:

Add 2 tablespoons of butter to a medium skillet and cook shrimp and raw fish over medium heat until fish turns white (about 3 minutes), add salt and pepper, 2 tablespoons of pesto, and the smoked salmon and saute for 1-2 more minutes to evenly coat the seafood in the pesto.

Preheat oven to 400 degrees. Spread 2 tablespoons of pesto sauce evenly across the pizza crust. Spread ¼ cup of Italian 4-cheese blend and then layer spinach evenly across. Add mushrooms and tomatoes. Next, layer in the seafood evenly across the entire pizza and top with the remaining ¾ cup of Italian 4-cheese blend. Place in the oven and cook for 15-16 minutes or until the edges of the crust are browned and the cheese is melted. Let the pizza cool for 1-2 minutes and then cut and serve. Enjoy with your favorite salad!

Red Beans And Rice

This popular southern dish is great for those cool fall nights when a steaming bowl of beans and rice is the perfect comfort food. A Louisiana staple, this dish was made on Mondays using Sunday's leftover ham hock. I remember the first time I tried Red Beans and Rice, I was visiting friends in New Orleans, and it was love at first bite!

If you've always wanted to make this dish but don't like the thought of having to soak the beans overnight, I've included a quick soak method that only takes one hour, so what are you waiting for? Bon appétite!

Makes 6 servings

Ingredients:

- 1 pound dry red kidney beans
- 1 pound andouille sausage (or kielbasa sausage) sliced
- 2 cups cubed ham (from ham steak or add a ham hock into the pot)
- 2 bay leaves
- 10 cups water (or chicken stock if you don't want to use ham)
- 3 celery stalks, diced
- 1 large yellow onion, chopped
- 1 green or red bell pepper, chopped
- 3-4 cloves garlic, minced
- 2 tablespoons fresh parsley, coarsely chopped
- 2 tablespoons of butter
- 2 teaspoons of thyme, roughly chopped
- 2 teaspoons Tony Chachere Creole Seasoning, to taste
- Pinch of cayenne pepper
- ½ teaspoon of salt
- ½ teaspoon of pepper
- 2 green onions, diced, for garnish
- Several dashes hot sauce, to each bowl when serving (optional)
- 6 cups cooked rice (to serve)

Directions:

1. In a large stockpot, add red kidney beans and cover with room temperature water. Allow to soak overnight (12-14 hours) before making the beans. OR use this quick soak method: Place the clean dried beans in a pot and cover with room

temperature water. Place over medium heat and bring to a boil. As soon as the beans boil, cover, remove from heat, and allow to soak for 1 hour. Continue on with the recipe.

2. Drain water from beans. In a large stockpot, combine beans, bay leaves, and 10 cups of water or chicken stock. Bring to boil; 30 minutes, stirring occasionally.

3. In a large saucepan, add butter, celery, green or red pepper, and chopped onions and saute over medium heat for about 6 minutes. Then add diced andouille sausage and brown over medium heat, stirring occasionally, about 4 minutes. Add in garlic and ham and cook 2 minutes more. Add this mixture to the pot of red beans.

4. Reduce heat on pot of beans to medium-low and simmer, uncovered, about 2 hours, stirring occasionally. Beans should thicken in the pot.

5. With 30 minutes remaining, add in remaining seasonings and fresh parsley and thyme. Continue to cook until the beans are tender and creamy. If you find that the beans are still too watery, simply keep cooking until the mixture is very thick and almost paste-like.

6. Remove from the heat. Remove the bay leaves.

7. Place 1 cup of cooked rice in each bowl. Add several dashes of hot sauce to each (optional). Spoon beans over the rice. Garnish with chopped green onions on top.

∽

Ruthie's Ragin' Cajun

This recipe is named after my mother, Ruth, who came up with this tasty dish that's so easy to make it might quickly become one of your favorites. It's a great recipe for busy moms who want to spend less time cooking and more time enjoying a delicious and healthy meal with the family at the dinner table. It gets its Cajun influence as a spin-off of red beans and rice, though the beans and spices in this dish give it a totally unique flavor that makes it one of our family's favorite meals.

Total cook time: 20 mins. Makes 4 servings.

Ingredients: Makes 4 servings

- 1 lb. of your favorite pork sausage (hot or mild, depending on how spicy you like it)
- 1 15 oz can of black beans (drained)
- 1 12 oz can of Ro-Tel
- 1 teaspoon of Italian Seasoning
- 1 teaspoon of jalapeno juice (optional)
- Instant brown or white rice (4 servings)

Directions:

1. Brown pork sausage in a large skillet over medium-high heat, about 5-7 minutes.
2. Add Italian seasoning, black beans, Ro-Tel, and jalapeno juice. Stir well, cover with lid, and reduce heat to low. Simmer for 15 minutes.
3. Cook instant rice according to package instructions.

4. Once meat and rice are ready, add a cup of rice into each bowl and then scoop the Ragin' Cajun mixture on top. And voila, there you have it—an easy, delicious, and hearty meal that will satisfy your family and give you more time to enjoy together!

Oysters Rockefeller

This appetizer is so rich and delicious I'm guessing it got it's name after the richest man of the day, John D. Rockefeller —and it's a lot easier to make than you might think. A rich, creamy blend of spinach, bacon, and delicious cheeses over plump oysters is then baked to perfection. It's so yummy!

My lifelong love affair with this dish began on one of my trips to visit family in New Orleans. I went to eat at Antoine's, where the original Oysters Rockefeller recipe was created by the founder's son, Jules Alciatore, back in the late 1800s. I did a little checking around, and rumor has it that Jules snuck his original recipe to the grave with him.

Of course, plenty of folks have tried to recreate his rich, savory dish which is why there are so many versions available to try at your favorite restaurants. This is my modification from several recipes that I've tried over the years. I hope you enjoy this classic dish as much as I do!

Makes 24 appetizers

Ingredients:

- 2 dozen oysters, shucked and in the half shell

- 3 slices cooked bacon, chopped
- 15 oz fresh baby spinach, finely chopped (1.5 bags – 10 oz size)
- 5 tablespoons butter
- 1½ shallots, finely chopped
- 3 tablespoons fresh parsley, finely chopped
- 2-3 garlic cloves, minced
- 2 tablespoons white wine
- 2 tablespoons heavy cream
- ½ teaspoon of Pernod (optional)
- ½ cup of Parmesan or Italian 4-cheese blend
- ½ cup Panko bread crumbs
- Lemon wedges for garnish
- Rock salt

Directions:

1. Carefully shuck oysters using an oyster knife or purchase them shucked and in the half shell. Set aside and keep cool.
2. Preheat oven to 450° F.
3. Melt the butter in a pan and sauté shallots and garlic over medium heat for one minute. Add the chopped spinach and cook another two minutes until the spinach has wilted.
4. Add the white wine and Pernod (optional) to vegetables and cook another two minutes, stirring constantly.
5. Add the cream and stir until well combined. This mixture can be stored in the refrigerator for 3 days if you want to prepare it ahead of time.

6. Beat the mixture with an electric mixer to evenly combine ingredients and infuse air for a fluffy texture.

7. In a large oven pan with edges, add a layer of rock salt on the bottom and place oysters in half shell evenly in the pan (the salt will stabilize the oysters so they don't tip over while cooking).

8. Spoon the spinach mixture evenly over each oyster to the edge of the shells.

9. Top each oyster with bacon crumbles and a sprinkle of parsley.

10. Combine the Parmesan or Italian cheese blend with panko bread crumbs and scatter evenly over the top of oysters.

11. Place in oven and cook for 15-20 minutes, watching carefully, until the topping bubbles and is lightly browned.

12. Remove from oven and use a spatula to carefully transfer to a serving plate—these will be extremely hot, so handle with caution.

13. Serve immediately with lemon wedges.

Oyster Casserole

If you are looking for a unique and delicious casserole to serve during the holidays, try this southern classic. The blend of oysters, mushrooms, cheese, and sauces makes it mouth-watering and unforgettable. I wouldn't be surprised if it becomes one of your favorite holiday dishes too!

I discovered this recipe online last year and modified it slightly because my family loves mushrooms, garlic, and bacon. I highly recommend you visit howtofeedaloon.com to see the instructional video for this recipe because Kris and Wesley are the most fabulous cooks and hosts, and their videos are a hoot!

*Adapted from the original recipe: howtofeedaloon.com | Kris Longwell | Oyster Casserole

Ingredients:

- 2 16 oz containers of fresh oysters, drained and rinsed
- 3 pieces of bacon; crumbled
- 2 tablespoons olive oil
- 6 tablespoons of butter, divided
- 10 oz of mushrooms, sliced
- 4 cloves of garlic, minced
- ½ cup of celery, chopped
- ½ cup yellow onion, chopped
- ½ cup red bell pepper, seeded and chopped
- ½ cup scallions, white and green parts, sliced
- ½ cup grated Parmesan cheese
- 1 cup of breadcrumbs from a loaf of bread, chopped with crust removed
- 2 tablespoons all-purpose flour
- ½ cup of half and half
- 1 tablespoon fresh lemon juice
- 1 tablespoon Worcestershire sauce
- 1 tablespoon hot sauce
- 1 teaspoon Kosher salt
- 1 teaspoon freshly ground black pepper

Directions:

1. Preheat oven to 400° F.
2. Heat the olive oil in a large skillet over medium-high heat. Add two tablespoons of butter and stir until melted. Add yellow onion, celery, and red bell pepper and cook until tender and translucent, about 5-7 minutes. Add scallions and garlic and cook for one more minute.
3. Add well-drained oysters and mushrooms to the mixture and bring to a simmer, stirring frequently. Cook for five minutes and then set aside.
4. In a medium saucepan, melt 2 tablespoons of butter over medium heat. Whisk in flour, and cook, whisking constantly for 1 minute until smooth. Then stir in half and half, Worcestershire sauce, lemon juice, hot sauce, salt, and pepper, whisking constantly to keep it from burning. Cook for 2-5 minutes more until the roux is very thick and begins to bubble.
5. Stir in the Parmesan cheese and cook until melted, about 1 more minute.
6. Using a colander or fine-mesh sieve, strain the oyster and mushroom mixture. Then add the oyster mixture to the cheese sauce and stir until fully incorporated.
7. Melt the remaining 2 tablespoons of butter and toss the bread crumbs in the butter with a dash of salt. Set aside.
8. Spread the mixture evenly in a 11X7 inch baking dish. Top with crumbled bacon.

9. Sprinkle the bread crumbs with butter evenly on top of the oyster mixture.

10. Bake for 15 minutes or until bubbling. Then place the dish on the broiler rack and broil for 1-2 minutes, until the topping is lightly browned. Remove from the oven and serve while hot.

Killer Seafood Gumbo

Recipe submitted by Martin Brooks

If you love gumbo as much as I do and you want to learn how to make this classic dish, you're in luck! Because this is honestly the best gumbo that I've ever had. This recipe is Martin Brook's adaptation of his Cajun grandmother's family recipe.

Several times a year, Martin finds himself preparing this recipe for a large group of friends. I was lucky enough to be invited over by Martin to cook this recipe with him, and the first bite I took was so delicious, I dubbed it "Killer Gumbo." I'm glad it found its way into the Savory Mystery Series and that he gave me permission to share it with you. I promise you won't be disappointed!

Makes 12 servings

Seafood Stock:
Ingredients:

- Heads and shells from 2 pounds of shrimp (bodies are used in Gumbo recipe)

- Snow crab bodies – 1 whole or 2 halves (crab legs are used in the Seafood Gumbo recipe)
- 1 can smoked oysters
- 2 bottles clam juice
- 4 stalks celery, broken into 4-inch pieces
- 4 carrots, cut in half
- 1 medium white onion, cut into fourths
- 1 gallon water
- 2 unpeeled cloves of garlic, crushed
- 2 bay leaves
- ¼ of a bunch of parsley, coarsely chopped
- ½ teaspoon of sweet basil
- ¼ teaspoon thyme
- 1 teaspoon salt
- ½ teaspoon black pepper

Seafood Stock Preparation Instructions:

1. Start this recipe by making the seafood stock. Place all the ingredients listed for this part in a large stockpot. Bring the pot to a slow boil and cook for about an hour until reduced to 3 quarts of liquid.
2. Remove from heat and allow to cool for 30 minutes at room temperature. Strain through a fine colander and discard the solids.
3. Refrigerate for 1 hour and skim off any foam or color that rises to the top.
4. Makes 3 quarts of stock for the Seafood Gumbo.

Seafood Gumbo:
Ingredients:

- 1 cup cooking oil
- 1¼ cups all-purpose flour
- 2 large chopped yellow onions
- 1 cup minced celery
- ⅔ cup chopped green bell pepper
- 3 cloves minced garlic
- 2 (15-ounce) cans petite diced tomatoes
- 2¼ quarts Seafood Stock (directions provided above)
- 2 bay leaves
- ½ teaspoon sweet basil
- ¼ teaspoon thyme
- ½ teaspoon Tabasco sauce
- 2 teaspoons salt
- ½ teaspoon black pepper
- ½ teaspoon garlic powder
- 1 teaspoon onion powder
- ¼ teaspoon white pepper
- 1 tablespoon Worcestershire sauce
- 1 16 oz package frozen cut okra
- 3 tablespoons cooking oil
- 1 package frozen snow crabs, legs removed and cut into 3-inch pieces (bodies reserved for Seafood Stock recipe)
- 1 pint-sized container of crab meat (claw or body meat)
- 2 pounds large raw shrimp, peeled and deveined
- 1 pound andouille sausage, cut into half rounds and sauteed
- 2 cups oysters with liquid (freshly shucked or substitute with canned if you don't have access to fresh oysters)

- ½ cup finely chopped green onion
- ½ cup finely chopped fresh parsley
- file powder to taste (thickening agent that is made from ground-up sassafras)
- additional salt and pepper to taste can be added at the end
- 3 cups cooked white rice

Seafood Gumbo Preparation Instructions:

1. Once your seafood stock is ready, begin making the gumbo. In a heavy metal pot, heat the cup of cooking oil over medium heat. Add the flour and cook over low to medium heat until you get a dark brown roux, stirring constantly to avoid burning.
2. When the desired color is reached, add the onions, celery, bell pepper, okra, and garlic and sauté for 7 minutes.
3. Then add the canned tomatoes. Cook for 3-5 minutes, then add the Seafood Stock, bay leaves, sweet basil, thyme, Tabasco sauce, salt, black pepper, garlic powder, onion powder, white pepper, and Worcestershire sauce and bring to a boil.
4. Once the dish has come to a boil, reduce the heat to low, cover with lid, and simmer the gumbo for 1½ hours covered.
5. During the final 20 minutes of simmering time, add the following ingredients: crab leg pieces, crab meat, shrimp, sauteed sausage, oysters, green onions, and parsley.

6. After the gumbo has simmered for 1½ hours covered, check seasonings and adjust salt and pepper to taste.
7. Pour into individual serving bowls and add a pinch of the file powder and a couple of tablespoons of the cooked white rice.
8. Cooking tip: If your gumbo ends up slightly salty, add a whole, peeled potato to the soup and simmer for about 15 minutes to absorb salt. Remove the potato and serve.

～

"As Good as Your Mama's" Creole Jambalaya
Recipe and introduction submitted by Darci Heikkinen

If you want an authentic Creole jambalaya, this recipe will make you think you're in New Orleans. This "red" jambalaya, so-called by the addition of tomatoes, makes a moist but thick dish—no soupy or gooey jambalaya here.

I enjoy making this recipe for my family, but I have easily doubled (and tripled it) to serve at Mardi Gras celebrations. But don't think you have to wait until Fat Tuesday—you can enjoy this fabulous dish any day of the year! Also, check out some ideas for a vegetarian option below. You might be surprised at how you don't miss the meat.

Ingredients

- 1 pound chicken thighs (I prefer boneless and skinless, or you can use rotisserie chicken to speed things up)
- 2 tablespoons unsalted butter

- 1 pound Andouille sausage, sliced into rounds (or try chorizo or other smoked sausage)
- 1 medium yellow onion, chopped
- 1 green pepper, chopped
- 2 celery stalks, diced
- 1 bunch green onions, chopped (separate the white and green parts)
- 3 cloves garlic, minced
- 1 (28 oz) can crushed tomatoes
- ¼ cup tomato puree (or use 3 tablespoons tomato paste + 6 tablespoons water)
- 2 whole bay leaves
- 1 teaspoon salt
- ½ teaspoon ground black pepper
- ¼ teaspoon ground cayenne
- ¼ teaspoon dried thyme
- 1 teaspoon Creole seasoning (I prefer Tony Chachere)
- 4 cups chicken stock
- 1 tablespoon Louisiana pepper sauce (not hot sauce) or ¼ teaspoon red pepper flakes, more to taste
- 2 cups long-grain white rice (make sure you rinse very well to prevent mushy jambalaya)

Directions:

1. Heat 1 ½ tablespoons oil in large skillet over medium heat. Add chicken thighs, cook for 5 minutes.
2. Flip chicken and continue to cook for 6-7 more minutes or until no longer pink. Remove from

skillet and let drain of excess oil. When cool, shred chicken and set aside.

3. Melt butter in a large stockpot or Dutch oven set over medium-high heat. Brown Andouille sausage on both sides.

4. Stir in onions, green pepper, celery, white parts of green onions, and garlic. Stir occasionally and cook about 5 minutes or until onions are translucent.

5. Add crushed tomatoes, tomato puree, salt, pepper, cayenne, thyme, Creole seasoning, and bay leaf. Stir 2 minutes.

6. Add shredded chicken and chicken stock and stir to combine. Stir in pepper sauce or red pepper flakes.

7. Bring to a boil then reduce to a simmer. Cook uncovered until liquid is reduced by ⅓ or about 1 hour.

8. Bring jambalaya to a boil. Stir in 2 cups uncooked rice then reduce heat to medium. Stirring occasionally, cook 15–25 minutes, or until rice is done (if rice is not done and liquid is gone, stir in ¼ cup water at a time).

9. Stir in remaining green onions. Serve and enjoy!

Other variations you might like to try...

- Want shrimp? Add ¾ pound raw shrimp, peeled and deveined: When jambalaya is nearly cooked, lay the shrimp on the top and gently mix through to cover. Let cook until shrimp are pink, approximately 5–7 minutes.

- Need a vegetarian option? Omit the meat, and replace with carrots, zucchini, eggplant, and okra. Cook ½ cup carrot (sliced or diced) with the onions, green pepper, and celery. Add in 1 medium zucchini (chopped) and 1 small eggplant (chopped) with the tomatoes. Add about 1 cup okra (sliced into rounds, fresh or frozen) during the last 5–10 minutes of cooking. Prefer another vegetable? Feel free to experiment here, but don't automatically discount the okra (it's better than you think). You can also try adding in vegetarian sausage or red beans if you want.

Crab Cakes

These crab cakes are so delicious and filling they're criminal! What makes this recipe so good is that it's simple and yet full of flavor. Moist, tender crab with the perfect amount of seasoning then coated in panko makes this a dish you will savor every time. And this is an easy meal to make when you don't have a lot of time to cook. These crab cakes also make for a savory appetizer when you have guests over for dinner. I've experimented with several recipes over the years, and this combination is worthy of sharing. I hope you enjoy it as much as we do!

Makes 8 crab cakes
Ingredients:

- 1pound fresh crab meat (pick over for any remaining bits of shell)

- 2 eggs, beaten
- 1 cup panko breadcrumbs (you can substitute for a full sleeve of crackers)
- ¼ cup oil for frying
- 1 teaspoon Old Bay Seasoning
- ¼ cup green onion; finely diced (can substitute with 1 tablespoon dill for a milder flavor)
- ¼ cup red bell pepper; finely diced
- ¼ cup celery; finely diced
- 1 tablespoon freshly chopped Parsley
- ¼ cup mayonnaise
- 2 tablespoons Dijon mustard
- ½ teaspoon Tabasco or hot sauce
- 2 teaspoons Worcestershire sauce
- 1 teaspoon ground pepper
- Salt to taste
- Lemon wedges
- Tartar sauce or Cajun-style ranch for serving

Directions:

1. In a medium mixing bowl, combine crab meat, parsley, Old Bay Seasoning, green onion, celery, red peppers, and panko crumbs and mix together.
2. In a second mixing bowl, combine eggs, mayonnaise, Dijon, Worcestershire, hot sauce, pepper, and salt. Mix well. Then combine with the crab meat mixture.
3. Divide the mixture to form 8 crab patties about 1 inch thick.

4. Heat oil in a large skillet on medium heat. Fry crab cake patties for 4-5 minutes on each side or until they are golden brown.

5. Serve with lemon wedges and tartar sauce or a Cajun-style ranch

Quick and Savory Beef and Kale Skillet

If you are looking for an easy delicious dinner meal, this Beef and Kale Savory Skillet fits the bill and will delight your tastebuds with its unique flavors. My family loves this tasty meal, and I love making it for them because it's so quick and easy!

This dish doesn't require too many ingredients, and there is very little prep, so you can have dinner on the table in less than thirty minutes. It's also very hearty, so you can eat it alone or pair it with a simple salad and a glass of red wine. I hope this becomes one of your family's favorites too!

Makes 4 servings

Ingredients:

- 1 pound of ground beef (80/20)
- 1 15oz can white beans (Navy or Great Northern)
- 7 cups kale (rinsed, stalks removed, and chopped)
- 1 cup of Parmesan cheese or Italian 4-cheese blend
- 3 tablespoons extra virgin olive oil
- Juice from 1½ lemons

- 3 tablespoons sundried tomatoes, diced
- 2 cloves fresh garlic minced (optional)
- 2 tablespoons Cajun Trinity (with garlic) seasoning
- 3 teaspoons cumin
- ⅛ teaspoon of cayenne
- 3 teaspoons oregano, dry
- Salt and pepper to taste

Directions:

1. In an extra-large skillet or wok, heat olive oil over medium heat, then add sundried tomatoes and garlic and sauté for two minutes
2. Add ground beef to skillet with Cajun Trinity, cumin, cayenne pepper, dried oregano, and salt and pepper. Cook for 2-3 minutes, until ground beef is browned.
3. Add the pre-washed and chopped kale and lemon juice, cover, lower heat to medium low and cook for five minutes. Kale should be wilted.
4. Remove the lid, raise heat back to medium and cook about 3 more minutes to evaporate the liquid.
5. Remove from the heat, sprinkle the cheese on top, and serve

Would you like more Piper Sandstone Adventures?

P.S. Thank you for reading my books. Writing is my passion, and I look forward to *your* feedback. Would you like to see more of Piper Sandstone's adventures in Savory?

If so, I'd like to ask for a small favor. Would you be so kind as to leave a review on Amazon? Your honest opinion is much appreciated because it helps me create my best work for you.

Thank you!
Karen

Scan the QR code below to Leave A Review:

FREE GIFT

Receive your FREE copy of **Hash Browns And Homicide**, the series prequel, and get notified via email of new releases, giveaways, contests, cover reveals, and insider fun when you sign up to my VIP mailing list!

Scan Barcode To Sign Up and Claim Your FREE Exclusive Book

BOOKS BY KAREN MCSPADE

The Savory Mystery Series

Hash Browns And Homicide

Murder and Grits

Red Beans And R.I.P.

Mystery On the Half Shell

Killer Gumbo

Crab Cake Criminal

Deep Fried Revenge Series

Bacon, Bodyguards, and Ballistics - Book 1

Bacon, Bodyguards, and Ballistics - Book 2

Bacon, Bodyguards, and Ballistics - Book 3

Bacon, Bodyguards, and Ballistics - Book 4

Bacon, Bodyguards, and Ballistics - Book 5

Crystal Beach Magic Mystery Series

Cat Scratch Murder

Claw of Attraction

Feline Like a Suspect

A Meowing Suspicion

Paws in Space

Scan the barcode to visit my Amazon Author page for a complete listing of my books.

ABOUT THE AUTHOR

Raised in the Arkansas River Valley, Karen McSpade grew up with a fishing pole in one hand and her trusty .410 shotgun in the other. Exploring the creeks and woods around her hometown while hunting with her father kept her "entertained and out of jail," as her mom likes to say.

As a child, her most prized possessions were her books and her Michael Jackson album collection. These led her to a brief venture into breakdancing and poetry slamming before discovering her true passion, bringing stories and characters to life. Today, she focuses on the two things that still inspire her creativity—her love for food and dishing up mysteries with a dash of humor.

Karen's novels feature compassionate and strong-willed leading ladies determined to uncover the truth and seek justice. She loves creating stories filled with mystery, romance, magic, and adventure that allow readers to join her characters on their journey, leaving behind the real world for a few hours at a time.

When she's not writing, Karen's favorite things are spending time with family, traveling, cooking, reading, gardening, and enjoying nature. She lives in Northwest Arkansas with her family and a very spoiled Wheaten Terrier who doubles as her writing assistant.

Scan the barcode to join Karen on Facebook for updates, fun, and prizes!